James Bong

Agent Of Anarchy

Todd Borho

James Bong

Premise: Anarchism, action, and comedy blended into a spoof of the James Bond franchise.

Setting:

Year: 2028

Principal Characters and Locations:

James Bong – Former MI6 asset for special operations. Now an anarchist committed to freeing people from statist hands. 30 years old, well built, steely gray eyes, dirty blond hair. Bong moves frequently.

K – Nerdy anarchist hacker in his early twenties based in Acapulco, Mexico.

Miss Moneybit – Feisty, attractive blogger in her late twenties and based in Washington, DC.

General Small - Bumbling and incompetent General. Former Army Intel and now with the CIA.

Sir Hugo Trax – MI6 officer who was involved in training and controlling Bong during Bong's MI6 days.

Episode 1 – Part 1

Scene 1

Bong is driving at a scorching speed down a desert highway in a black open-source 3D printed vehicle modeled after the Acura NSX.

K's voice: Bong!

Bong (narrows eyes at encrypted blockchain based smartwatch): K, what the hell? I had my watch off!

K (proud, sitting in his ridiculously overstuffed highback office chair): I know, I turned it on remotely. I've got great news!

Bong (looking ahead at the cop car and the cop's victim on the side of the road): Kinda busy right now.

K (twirling in his chair): It can't wait! It's a go! It's a go! I'm so excited!

Bong (sarcastically): You're breaking up on me. What's that? You're gonna go and disappear out of my life forever? That is exciting! (clicks off smartwatch and smiles)

Bong has his speed up to 150mph and aims the car as close as possible to the cop without hitting him. The cop is approaching the other vehicle just as Bong whips by.

Cop (hair blowing from wind): What the hell!

Bong smiles smugly and activates the nitrous. The chubby cop fumbles his way back to his car and takes off after Bong. The relieved driver of the other car drives off contentedly after avoiding the cop's extortion attempt.

Scene 2

After evading the cop, Bong has taken refuge at a bar called Bootlegger overlooking Lake Tahoe.

K's voice: Bong!

Bong (grimaces at smartwatch): Right, you again. You know that Kay is a woman's name, right? And what happened to you disappearing, anyway? That would make me very happy.

K: While you were busy being an intolerable ball of swine puss, I was busy getting funds for the big mission we talked about. What were you doing, anyway?

Bong: I was stopping a control freak in a costume from violently extorting a free human.

K: What's all that chatter? And I hear 80s pop music. Are you in a bar right now?

Bong: Yes, did you call to live vicariously through me? You could go out once in a while, you know.

K: Get somewhere private.

(Bong steps outside on an empty patio overlooking the lake)

K: Ok, that's better. So we've got enough Stashcoin to get Ross Mulbricht out.

Bong (smiling contentedly to himself): We should talk about this in person. Don't say another word.

K: You don't trust my encryption?

Bong: I don't trust your ego. (clicks smartwatch off)

Scene 3

Acapulco, Mexico. K meanders into his kitchen.

Bong: Love what you've done with the place.

K (shouts, startled, clutches chest): Why do you do that!? Can't you knock?

Bong: I can, but it's not as pleasurable. I took the liberty of making coffee.

K: How thoughtful.

Bong: I put some rum in mine. You really should spend money on the top shelf. It makes a huge difference. So tell me the details about Mulbricht.

K (pouring coffee for himself): You know how I hate to brag, but thanks to my genius, you have to do very little.

Bong: Where'd you get the funds?

K: Donations.

Bong (pleased): I'm listening.

K: Ok, logistics. Mulbricht is in the high security federal prison in Florence, Colorado. He's on the third level in cell 33.

Bong: Those masonic bastards.

K: Tell me about it. So I've got private jets lined up to and fro. One chartered from SteemAir and the other from Swarm City.

Bong: With no pilot.

K: Exactly.

Bong: And no autonomous functions?

K: I know you only fly yourself because you're so damned paranoid.

Bong: Paranoia helps keep me alive.

K: Don't get close to their airspace.

Bong (cold and incredulous): Don't tell me how to do my job. How about cars?

K: Well, you've got your car, right?

Bong: I'm not using my car for this operation.

K; Well, hmmm. Ok, I've got it. I had planned the throwaway vehicle to be a 1977 Trans Am.

Bong: It would be a shame to lose such a cherry.

K: Agreed. I suppose I could find a racing bike cheap enough for the getaway and then ditch that.

Bong: Now you're thinking.

K: Now about getting in.

Bong: Guns, brains, and balls usually work.

K: True enough, but this is high security and we don't want to draw too much attention right off the bat, now do we? Wait until you see what I've got for you. (motions Bong to follow into the next room)

The room is piled to the ceiling with gadgets and gizmos. Bong stands in awe of the techno-mess.

K (handing Bong a tiny black case, resembling a jewelry box): Go ahead, open it.

Bong (smirking): I had no idea you felt this way.

K (rolling eyes): I finally had the huevos to tell you.

Bong (opening box): Contacts? I can see just fine, thanks very much. Have you gone mad?

K: They're not just any old contacts. They're iris print contacts. All you have to do is approach some of the security personnel at the prison, look them in the eye for a second, and these will grab their iris print. Then you'll have access, and all without bloodshed, hopefully.

Bong: And for the cell?

K: Laser cutter.

Bong (impressed): How did you get this stuff? This is stuff that usually only the military has.

K: Silk Highway on the Substratum network.

Bong: How ironic. The free market website that Mulbricht was imprisoned for is still running and is helping to let him free.

K: I thought you'd appreciate that.

Bong: Which is why it cost a fortune to get all this together. Next level gear like this doesn't come cheap.

K (sighing deeply): Tell me about it. The price we pay for doing the right thing.

Bong: You're sure you weren't tracked doing all this?

K (cocky): You'll find out when you get there.

Bong (narrows eyes): And I'm flying him all the way back here?

K: I thought you didn't want me telling you how to do your job.

Bong folds arms and huffs.

K: That's on you. I'll be waiting to greet Mulbricht when he gets here.

Bong: And our little blogger is going to shine light on our valiant endeavors after it's all said and done?

K: She's chomping at the bit.

Bong: Good. She might come in handy some day.

K: What's that supposed to mean?

Bong (grimacing): Never mind. You're too simple minded to get it.

K: I can make your vehicles stop working at any moment. You know that, right?

Bong: Not before you meet your hero Ross Mulbricht.

K: The man has achieved martyr status and is still alive, which ranks high in my book. Not to mention he was a pioneer in the tech market and crypto.

Bong: When's all this supposed to go down?

K: Tomorrow at high noon.

Bong (chuckles): You're so melodramatic. It really is painful.

K: Just one more thing. How many people at that bar in Tahoe made stoner jokes about your name?

Bong: Harassing me never gets old for you, now does it? I don't even smoke cannabis!

K: Then maybe you should change your name. And you didn't answer my question.

Bong (reluctant voice): One girl asked.

K: Was she gorgeous?

Bong: Exquisite.

K (grinning ear to ear): All over?

Bong (satisfied smile): A gentleman never tells.

End Part 1

5

Episode 1 – Part 2

Scene 1

Bong, K, and Miss Moneybit are having a video conference. Miss Moneybit is in her apartment in DC. James and K are at K's house in Acapulco, Mexico.

Miss Moneybit (tapping fingers anxiously on desk): Helluva story, guys. I'll have it published within 24 hours. Too bad about the video, though.

Bong (holding ice pack on head, sighing): Yeah, I forgot the extra wearable camera, and my smartwatch was malfunctioning for some reason (looks at K disapprovingly). And to top it off, boy genius here hacked the security cameras in the prison, shut them off, and then got cocky and tried to record using their equipment.

K (cuts Bong off): I did record with their equipment, it just backfired a bit.

Bong: A bit? They have me on camera now, breaking Ross Mulbricht out of prison, and we don't have any video for ourselves! How does that qualify as only a bit? What the hell were you thinking?

K: Without the video, it won't get nearly as many hits online. I was just trying to cover your ass. You're the one who forgot the extra camera. Are you sure you're not a stoner?

Bong (rolls eyes): Quite.

Miss Moneybit: Ok, boys, settle down. A print story will have to do. I have some pressing questions.

Bong: I hate getting grilled.

K: Even when it's a super rare anarchist babe like her?

Miss Moneybit: You're pathetic. So where is Mulbricht now?

K: That's classified.

Miss Moneybit: Give it a rest.

Bong: I hate to agree with him, but we really can't disclose his location.

Miss Moneybit: Why not?

Bong: A little thing called privacy. Next question.

Miss Moneybit: Bong, how'd you hurt your head?

(K starts laughing out loud, nudges Bong on arm)

K: Go ahead, tell her.

Scene 2

Scene flashes back to Bong and Mulbricht's escape from prison. They're running full speed in the Colorado countryside attempting to make it to their escape plane. They're being pursued by control freaks in blue costumes…..aka…cops.

Mulbricht (yelling): This might be the worst prison break ever!

(Bong, panting, ignores the insult)

Mulbricht: Have you done this before?

Bong: You're not helping!

Mulbricht: You didn't answer my question!

Bong: No, I haven't!

Mulbricht: Great! Goodbye!

Bong: What?

Mulbricht: We're gonna die! I should've stayed in prison!

They approach the Cessna Turboprop that awaits them.

Bong: Just get in the plane and stop whining!

Mulbricht: I'm supposed to fly with you now? Ahhhhhh!

Mulbricht jumps into the plane in one speedy swoop. Bong attempts to do the same, but clips his head on the body of the plane as he jumps in.

Bong (anguish): Ahhhhh, my head! Son of a bitch!

Mulbricht (sad): Well, it was a decent life. Short, but decent.

Bong maneuvers some controls and the plane starts speeding down a field and gets into the air.

Scene 3

Scene flashes back to the video conference. Miss Moneybit and K are laughing hysterically.

Miss Moneybit: I can't believe you used to be a real spy!

K: And he claims he was at the top of his class!

Bong: I could snap your neck right now.

Miss Moneybit: Ok, ok, moving on. I don't understand something. Why did you get a turboprop? Aren't those small and dreadfully slow?

Bong: Thank you! Preachin to the choir! Mr. Cheapskate Supreme here went low brow on the equipment! Your frugality nearly cost me my life along with Mulbricht's, ya bloody little fool.

K: Hey, we were on a shoestring budget, what can I say?

Bong: Bullocks!

K: That was a sweet racing bike you had for the initial getaway.

Bong: Oh yeah, real sweet. It was like the first bike ever built and got a flat tire after about 2 minutes.

K (throws hands in air): Not my fault. You should've driven more carefully.

Bong: It was a prison break!

Miss Moneybit: Ok, ok. So when can I talk to Mulbricht?

K: When he's ready, I imagine. Want me to give him your number?

Miss Moneybit: You don't have my number and I would never give it to you, K.

Bong: I'll give it to Mulbricht if you'd like.

Miss Moneybit: Yes, please do.

K (frowning): Why does Bong get your number?

Miss Moneybit: Cuz he's hot, and not a lonely little pasty hacker like you. Another question.

K: Hold on. I've got a question for you before you fire off anymore at us. How much compensation will we get for all this work?

Miss Moneybit: It's hard to say. I'll have it on a few different sites soon. I'll post on Steemit first. That post should get at least a thousand steem, I imagine.

Bong: And we split it 3 ways, equally, right?

Miss Moneybit (reluctant voice, twiddling thumbs): I'm not sure that's what we agreed upon.

Bong: Then I'm not sure you'll be getting anymore exclusive stories of my exploits.

Miss Moneybit (pouty face): Oh, fine. Now for my next question. What are you gonna do about the video? Surely, the feds are already on it.

Bong (looking angrily at K): Yeah, what are you going to do about that?

K: I think you should go destroy it.

Bong: I'm not going to destroy property, even if it is the fed's.

K: Why not?

Bong: Because it's wrong and immoral. Besides, they've probably got copies spread all over the network by now, so I think if anyone gets to it, you should.

K: Me? Why me?

Bong: Cuz you're a hacker and it was your fault!

K: I say we just let it go. What are they gonna do, anyway?

Bong: Oh, gee, I dunno. Now I'm gonna be on the most wanted list. But that's not the worst of it. This will eventually get back to my former employers at MI6.

Miss Moneybit (ponderous look on face): Why didn't you just wear a mask, or something?

(Bong and K look at each other, dumbfounded)

Miss Moneybit: Unreal. You boys didn't think to do that?

Bong (stands up): I need a drink.

Scene 4

Sir Hugo Trax and General Small are having a video conference. Trax is at MI6 headquarters in London and General Small is at CIA headquarters in Langley, Virginia.

Trax (looking at footage of Bong cutting open Mulbricht's cell with a laser cutter): Finally, you've done something well by getting me this footage. I was on the verge of firing you, ya know.

General Small (wiping sweat off his balding brow): You can't fire me.

Trax: Maybe not, but I know people who know some people who can fire you. And that would be a shame this close to getting your pension.

General Small: Back to Bong. What are ya gonna do about him?

Trax: He busted out a prisoner in your territory. He's your problem, not mine. However, I know what a bumbling fool you can be at times, so in my own interest of self-preservation, I'll help you take care of Mr. Bong.

General Small (chewing loudly): Who else do you want in on this op? And what to do about the video? Make copies or destroy it?

Trax: No copies! Bong has been off the radar for 5 years and now resurfaces with a bang like this! I want as few as possible knowing about this, otherwise it could mean both our hides. And what are you eating now?

General Small: Late night pizza snack, the usual. And what to do with Bong? Could we turn him?

Trax (swirling his finger in a tropical green drink with an umbrella): He'll have to die, of course.

General Small: Are you drinking in the morning again?

Trax's eyes widen at the sight of a woman behind General Small.

Trax: Who the hell is that?

General Small (looks behind him): Oh, that? Don't worry, that's just the cleaning lady and she doesn't speak English.

Trax does facepalm.

Trax: Damn you, Small! Now we have to kill her, too!

Cleaning lady screams and runs out the door.

General Small (yelling at cleaning lady): I thought you don't speak English!

End Episode 1

Episode 2 – Part 1

Scene 1

It's been 10 days since Bong liberated Ross Mulbricht from the cage in Colorado. Bong is playing blackjack at a casino in Panama and losing badly.

K: Bong!

Bong (startled): Why don't I just leave this infernal smartwatch somewhere else?

K: Sorry to disturb your lackluster showing at the tables, but I've got great news!

Bong (talking to dealer): I'm afraid a pressing matter has come up.

Dealer: More pressing than losing your shirt at blackjack?

A grimacing Bong walks away.

K: You should learn to count cards like me, then you might win a hand or two.

Bong (looking around, paranoid): Could you not say stuff like that while I'm walking around a casino?

K: Come on, you're James Bong. What could happen?

Bong: I'd rather not find out.

K: Just get back to my place quick. And don't say goodbye to that groupie you were with last night, either. I don't trust her.

Bong: How do you know what I did last night?

K (twirling proudly in his highback, overstuffed office chair): You drunk dialed me and told me everything.

Bong: Bullocks! You were spying on me!

K (feigning panic): Um, sorry, can't hear ya. Getting too much interference. Gotta go now!

(CLICK)

Scene 2

Bong casually strolls into K's house in Acapulco the next morning, unannounced.

Bong: What's that giant dispenser with black liquid?

K (startled): Damnit, can you knock!?

Bong: You have your tricks, and I have mine.

K: It's a coffee dispenser.

Bong (amused): A coffee dispenser. How quaint.

K: Gotta keep the heart pumpin somehow.

Bong: You could go outside and exercise. So what's the marvelous news that's so damned urgent.

K: We're a hit!

Bong: What do you mean, we?

K: News of our mission to free Ross spread like wildfire! We made over 2,000 dollars on Steemit alone!

Bong: Great! So I can go back to the casino.

K (chagrined): Take a look at this. (Hits a key on his laptop and the image of an old couple on their front porch overlooking their farm goes on the wall)

Bong: You made me fly up here to look at your grandparents?

K: This handsome, hard working couple is about to lose the farm.

Bong: How's that?

K: They're behind on their taxes and the IRS is about to swoop in and steal it.

Bong: Can't you just fry the IRS computers and be done with it?

K: I could, but hacking exploits aren't as popularly received by netizens.

Bong: Damn new age techie lingo.

K: You get what I mean. Your exploits are much more entertaining, more popular, and thus, more profitable. You see where I'm going with this?

Bong: Yeah, I'm risking my life again while you fry your nerves on coffee and watch from a safe distance.

K: Come on, you can't live without this stuff! You were made for this!

Bong: I don't appreciate your choice of words. Miss Moneybit has agreed to the same terms of profit sharing after the dust settles?

K: Yep. And she said the profit could be more than double this time if we get video, so don't fudge that up like you did last time.

Bong: When and where?

K: 48 hours in North Dakota.

Bong: North Dakota in October?

K: Stop whining, it's not that cold up there yet.

(Conversation is interrupted by female voice)

Miss Moneybit: Why don't you swap places then, tough guy?

K (confused, then startled as he sees Miss Moneybit's face appear on the screen): Hey, how long have you been listening?

Miss Moneybit: Long enough to roll my eyes at you a dozen times.

K: And how'd you get access to my network?

Miss Moneybit (gleeful): You're not the only one with hacking skills. (Her giant face on the wall turns to Bong) Bong, we need to talk.

Bong: No we don't.

Miss Moneybit: Two things. First of all, get some footage of the old couple before the IRS parasites show up.

Bong (crossing arms): If I feel it necessary to speak with them, I will. Next.

Miss Moneybit: I need you to come to DC as soon as possible so we can talk in person, without your little sidekick there hanging on my every word.

Bong (throws arms in air): I'm not going out with you. We've been over this.

Miss Moneybit: Your ego looks bigger than the last time we spoke. Seriously, after this job, come see me.

Bong: You'll pay for transport?

Miss Moneybit: You're such a cheapskate.

Bong: I'll think about it. Say goodbye to your drooling admirer. (turns to K, who is fawning at the image of Miss Moneybit)

Miss Moneybit: We'll be in touch. Figuratively, I mean. I'd never touch you.

(CLICK)

K: She'll come around one day.

Bong: You shouldn't lie to yourself.

Scene 3

Bong is approaching the farm in a black helicopter.

Bong: At least it's flat, good for landing. (Suddenly, he hears a loud bang)

Bong: Are they shooting at me? Looks like my skills aren't needed here. I'd better land and approach on foot.

(Bong lands far from the handsome, bright white farmhouse, and sends an assortment of farm animals scurrying in all directions)

Bong: K, is the camera working?

K (sitting at his computer command center, chomping on some Cap'n Crunch): Did they shoot at you?

Bong (cringing): I'll take that as a yes.

Bong walks slowly with his hands up as he crosses a vast grass field on the approach to the farmhouse. Two figures are coming towards him.

Bong (shouting): Beautiful place you've got here!

(Another shot rings out)

Bong: I'm here to help!

Old male voice shouts back: That's what all those government goons say! This is private property!

Bong: I'm not from the government! Please don't shoot me!

They come to within 20 feet of each other. The old couple is eyeing Bong suspiciously. They're both holding shotguns.

Old man (pointing gun at Bong): State your business!

Bong (hands up in air, answers awkwardly): Well, um, let's see. How can I explain this?

Old woman: Spit it out, son! I was busy fixin lunch!

Bong: You see, the IRS is going to come in less than an hour, and I've come to help you fend them off.

Old man: And how the hell do you know that?

Bong: I can't say, really. You'll just have to trust me.

Old woman (with mocking laugh): Ah, trust him he says! A strange man in a black helicopter. Sure, and I suppose you'd like to sell me a bridge, too!

Old man holds his hand up to calm his wife.

Old man: If you can answer one question correctly, then we'll trust you.

Bong: Go ahead, shoot.
Old man: Bad choice of words!

(Bong cringes)

Old man: What is the definition of anarchy?

Bong (exhaling from relief): Without rulers!

Old man and old woman smile at each other and start walking towards Bong.

Old man: Hey, wait a minute! You look familiar. Are you that guy from the home gym infomercial?

Bong: I didn't even know those still existed.

Old woman (excited): No, dear! It's that guy that freed Ross! It's James Bong!

Old man: By golly, you're right! (extends hand to shake) We saw you on Steemit! Sorry we didn't recognize you sooner.

Old woman: You see, he's got cataracts, and I'm no spring chicken, either.

Bong (holds hand up): All is forgiven. I get shot at all the time, really. Seriously, we have less than an hour until the IRS actually does show up to try and steal your house.

Old man: Those immoral rat bastards. I've got some surprises coming for 'em.

Bong: If you'd like, I'll fend them off myself, that way they won't hold you accountable for any forceful behavior.

Old man: You mean self defense?

Bong: I'm just saying that if you defend against them, they might come back later with greater violence. If I'm the only one fighting back, then they might just come after me.

Old man: Well, ok, give it a shot. But if you get into trouble, we'll come out blazin.

Bong: That's the spirit.

Old woman: Speaking of blazin, I say we have a quick blunt. How about it, Bong?

Bong (chuckling): Actually, I don't partake.

Old woman: Oh, I'm sorry.

Bong: No need to apologize. It's a common misconception. You two go on home and have lunch and I'll get prepped in the chopper.

Old man: Thank you, son.

End Part 1

Episode 2 Part 2

In this episode, James takes on IRS agents and has a surprise waiting for him in DC.

Scene 1:

James Bong is sitting in his black helicopter and awaiting the arrival of the IRS agents who will soon try to steal private property from an old farming couple.

K: Bong!

Bong (exhaling deeply): What now, K? Are they here?

K (laughing hard): You're not gonna believe these characters.

Bong: Put it on the chopper's gps screen.

A screen in the central console of the chopper lights up and reveals a low-end sedan cruising down the two-lane highway that approaches the property. There are two middle-aged men inside. One is chubby and bald with puffy cheeks and eyes. The other is thin, bald, has a handle-bar mustache and wears super-thick coke-bottle glasses.

Bong (grinning): K, it looks as if your scrawny arse could've handled these two.

K: They look like pedos!

Bong: They probably are. Where else could anyone like that find employment, right?

K: Anyway, they'll be there in less than 5 minutes.

Bong readies the chopper and monitors their approach. The sedan comes barreling down the driveway, then slams the brakes and parks on top of a flower bed. The chubby one stumbles slightly as he gets out of the car and they both strut their way towards the front door of the farmhouse.

Chubby Agent (muttering): Damn farmers.

Thin Agent (stroking mustache): Why do ya say that?

Chubby Agent: Cuz they usually have guns and are troublemakers.

Chubby Agent does loud and obnoxious cop knock on the front door of the old couple's home. Bong is in the chopper, watching and listening.

Old man answers the door with his wife behind him.

Old man: Good afternoon. We don't want any.

Agents look at each other cynically.

Chubby Agent: Hi. We're here from the IRS. May we step in for a moment?

Old Man: I think it might be better if you state your business from outside.

Thin Agent (slicks thin hair back, and holds up a document): We have an order here to seize this property due to tax delinquency. I must insist that we step inside.

Bong lifts the chopper in the air and heads towards the house.
Chubby Agent (confused): What's that noise?

Thin Agent (pushy, yelling at old couple): Where is that coming from?

Old couple shrug shoulders, feigning ignorance. The chopper appears above the house and hovers near the agents. The agents look up disgustedly.

Chubby Agent (whispering to other agent): Did the home office send a chopper to help us?

Thin Agent: Do we even have choppers?

Bong gets on megaphone and speaks down to the agents.

Bong: Is there a problem here, guys?

Chubby Agent (yelling up at Bong): Who the hell are you?

Bong: Bong, James Bong!

The agents look at each other and gulp.

Chubby Agent: We're here to seize this house for tax delinquency!

Bong: You mean steal it?!

Thin Agent: It's not stealing! It's appropriation!

Bong: I'll be clear and brief. What you're doing is wrong and immoral and in violation of Natural Law! Nobody has the right to tax another! They owe the IRS nothing, you will not take their property, and you will leave now!

Thin Agent (stroking mustache): Yeah, whatcha gonna do about it?

Bong: Look at your chest!

Thin Agent looks down and sees laser sight over his heart. He freaks out and runs back to the car.

Chubby Agent (shaking fist in air): We'll come back with heavy artillery of our own! Just you wait!

The chubby agent scurries back to the car, they take off, plow over more flowers, and leave a trail of dust behind.

Old couple comes out and waves up at Bong.

Old Man: Thanks Mr. Bong!

Old Lady: Come back again some day and we'll have another doobie!

Bong chuckles, waves, and flies off.

K: Well done, Bong! And now for your reward. You get a date with Miss Moneybit, you lucky dog. What's the spot you're meeting at?

Bong: Mockingbird's, I think, and it's not a date. I'd prefer not to go, really. What are we going to do about the old couple? The agents will come back with a heavier hand next time, you know.

K: I'm already on it. I'm going to help them set up a Cell411 group so they can get crowdsourced help next time.

Bong: Great. The more people do things like that, the sooner I can retire.

Scene 2 – An empty and dimly lit restaurant in the District Of Criminals called "Mockingbird's". Miss Moneybit is sitting in a corner booth waiting for Bong. Bong enters and cautiously surveys his surroundings.

Miss Moneybit: What are you gawking around for, James?

Bong: In my line of work, it pays to be cautious. I recommend you do the same.

He takes a seat opposite Miss Moneybit. She holds out her hand. He shakes it reluctantly and she clasps her other hand over his wrist and smartwatch as they shake.

Miss Moneybit: It's great to meet you in person!

Bong (gruffly): The feeling isn't mutual. We have a business relationship, and one I prefer to keep long distance.

Miss Moneybit: Well, thanks for coming, anyway. Some things are better to be done in person, you know?

Bong: So what's this all about? Why did you insist on meeting me here?

Miss Moneybit: It's a nice place, isn't it? I love the décor.

Bong: I wasn't referring to this shady looking restaurant. You have two minutes, then I'm out.

Miss Moneybit: Won't you have a drink with me?

Bong (looking around): No, I won't. I don't even see any service staff. You have 1 minute and 48 seconds.

Miss Moneybit: I want to deal with you directly from now on, and cut K out of the picture. I need your smartwatch contact info.

Bong (smirking): Not a chance.

Miss Moneybit: Why not? What do you need that little twerp for?

Bong: As much as I hate to admit it, he helps keep me low profile. His technical abilities are off the charts, despite his annoying demeanor and constant nagging.

Miss Moneybit: But then you'd get his share of the profit. And maybe I could set you up with another tech guru. Just think about it, please?

Bong: I wasn't finished. I don't trust you, either.

Miss Moneybit (shaking head in disbelief): The consummate spy, not trusting anyone.

Bong: Former spy. A healthy dose of skepticism can keep you alive, you know? Anyway, this little meeting is over. (stands up to leave) Don't ever request a meeting with me again unless it's actually important. (Walks off)

Miss Moneybit (calling out): If you change your mind, you know how to find me!

Bong ignores her and leaves. Two figures come out from the kitchen area behind Miss Moneybit.

Sir Hugo Trax: You did well, my dear.

Miss Moneybit: I didn't have much of a choice, did I?

General Small: Self preservation is a powerful motivator. Anyway, you shouldn't hang around with his type.

Miss Moneybit: And who should I hang around with?

General Small (head bobbling, grinning ear to ear): Well, I'm available tomorrow night.

Miss Moneybit (defiantly, standing to leave): I don't hang out with parasitic statist losers. (she walks off, then turns around just before heading out the door)

Miss Moneybit: It doesn't matter if you stop Bong, you know? You can't stop the human evolution to a voluntary society. (She leaves)

General Small: She'll come around.

Sir Hugo Trax: Don't give yourself false hope.

General Small: Should I have our squad follow Bong?

Sir Hugo Trax (sighing deeply): You simple fool. No, not yet. Bong's got to lead us to K first, then we're in business.

General Small: And what about Moneybit?

Sir Hugo Trax: We let her keep writing, as promised. Don't want to send up any red flags.

General Small: And after we get Bong and K?

Sir Hugo Trax: She'll have to die, of course.

General Small: Terrible to waste such a pretty young thing.

Sir Hugo Trax (eyes rolling): Enough of your fawning over that little anarchist tart. I won't let your desperation for female companionship fudge this operation.

General Small: Yes, sir.

Scene 3: Later that night, Bong is cruising along on a rural two-lane highway.

K: Bong!

Bong: Can't I get any peace?

K: It's an emergency.

Bong: Guess not.

K: I picked up an interference signal from your smartwatch.

Bong: It's not interfering enough. You still got through to me.

K: No, listen. I traced the signal and it went back to Langley. I don't know how, but they've got a lock on you in real time.

Bong (angry): That double crossing little.

(K cuts him off)

K: Let's not jump to conclusions. She wouldn't do this on her own initiative. They got her scared somehow.

Bong: Looks like I've got more work to do.

K: Whatever you do, don't come to my place right now.

Bong (grinning ironically): You know I do my best to avoid you at all costs.

K: So what's your next move?

Bong: Hanging up on you, then I'll have a drink.

Episode 3

Scene 1

K is at his happy hacker lair in Acapulco, swiveling in his oversized office chair, methodically sipping on a super jumbo coffee.

K: Bong! That bastard! I haven't heard from him in days! The least he could do is let me know if he's dead or not. (frowns) Who am I kidding? I'm just in anguish because I found someone I can't hack all the time. (glances at his toothpick arms) And being a pasty, socially inept skin-flint doesn't help either, I guess. (kicks his desk in frustration)

Scene 2

General Small is sitting at his desk at CIA headquarters. The desk is littered with pizza boxes, donut boxes, and candy wrappers. He's startled by one of his agents, who barges in without knocking.

General Small: Hey, ever heard of knocking? I could've been doing something top secret and important, ya know.

Agent: You could also lock the door.

General Small: So what's so urgent?

Agent: We got the trace back on Bong.

General Small: Excellent! Any idea on how we lost the signal in the first place?

Agent: Not a clue, sir. Does it really matter? We know where he is, so let's kill him and get this thing wrapped up.

General Small: Good point. Show me where he's at.

The agent punches some buttons on a tablet and a holographic map of DC pops up.

Agent: Do you see the flashing red letters that say "Murder, Death, Kill?"

General Small (munching on donut): Yep.

Agent: That's where he is. 123 Knockajaw Court. Should I send some specialists to neutralize him?

General Small: Not just yet. That address sounds familiar. How long has he been stationary?

Agent: Hell if I know. The signal just came back a few minutes ago.

General Small: Wait! Now I know! That's my address! My wife and children could be in danger!

Agent: Do you have sufficient life insurance on them?

General Small (rolling eyes): Of course.
Agent: Then what's the problem? I'll send the death squad right away.

General Small (pondering his options): You make a valid point, but I'd better at least attempt to get my family out first. I'll have to confront Bong myself.

Agent (laughing hysterically): Alone? You?

General Small: Why is that funny?

Agent: Because you're old and fat and Bong is young and one of the best trained secret agents in history. Need I continue?

General Small: You're dismissed. If you don't hear from me within an hour.

Agent cuts him off.

Agent: Yeah, yeah, I know, you're dead and I might get promoted.

General Small (getting up to leave): Oh, while I'm out, there should be another pizza arriving. If they don't have extra cheese on it this time, don't tip that lousy putz, ok?

Agent: I never tip anyway.

Scene 3

30 minutes later, General Small goes into his house and finds his wife and children bound and gagged on the floor with 3 men in black standing over them.

General Small: What the hell are you guys doing here?

Man In Black: We were called in from your office, sir.

General Small: Well it sure as hell wasn't me! Why is my family tied up?

Man In Black: Trying to get them to talk. You never know who to trust in this business.

General Small: It's my family, you oaf! Untie them now! And how the hell are they supposed to talk with their mouths taped off, anyway?

Man In Black (puzzled look): Good point, sir. (goes to untie the family)

General Small: Did you find anything regarding Bong? We know he was here at some point because of the signal.

Man In Black: Affirmative, sir. (holds out Bong's smartwatch) We found this on the front doorstep with a note, sir.

General Small: What did the note say?

Man In Black: Nothing.

General Small: What do you mean?
Man In Black: It's a picture (holds out paper in front of General Small's face)

General Small (grimacing): A laughing emoji graphic. Very clever, Bong. We'll see who gets the last giggle.

Man In Black: Last laugh, sir.

General Small (shouting, angry): Whatever!

Scene 4

Agent outside General Small's office is zoned out on his tablet. There's a knock at the door.

Male voice outside door: Pizza delivery!

Agent: Come in!

Door opens and James Bong steps in holding a pizza box. He's wearing a baseball cap, a terrible fake mustache, and glasses that make him look walleyed.

Agent (glancing up from tablet): About damn time!

24

Bong: This one is on the house.

Agent: Damn well better be! Go through that door and put it on the desk.

Bong (looking at the door curiously): You mean that door that says "Top Secret. Authorized Personnel Only"?

Agent (nonchalantly): Yep, that's the one.

Bong: Whatever you say, boss!

Bong enters General Small's office and shuts the door. He immediately sets the pizza on the table and then starts putting massive amounts of miniature surveillance equipment all over the office. After finishing and about to walk out, Bong is startled by the door swinging open.

Agent: Hey! What's taking you so long?

Bong: Oh, I was just awestruck by being in CIA headquarters, the bastion of freedom!

Agent: Yeah, I don't blame ya. It's tough guys like us that keep little people like you safe.

Bong: Thank you, sir.

Agent: Whatever. Out.

Bong leaves.

Agent (annoyed mumbling): Damn nobodies. Get a life, will ya?

Scene 5
Miss Moneybit comes into her apartment. She fixes herself a cocktail and starts lounging on the couch.

Bong: Don't scream.

Miss Moneybit turns around to see Bong standing in the doorway to her bedroom. She starts gulping air and flailing her arms, then adds a high pitched whining noise to the freak-out.

Miss Moneybit: Are you here to kill me?

Bong (smirking): If I were here to kill you, we wouldn't be talking right now. (starts eyeing the cocktail curiously) Is that a martini?

Miss Moneybit: Yep, can I make ya one?

Bong (grabbing glass off coffee table): Nope, yours will do just fine. (gulps it down to the last drop) Ahhhhh, that hit the spot! Now, on to business. I'll be gone in 2 minutes.

Miss Moneybit: Look, before you start (Bong waves his finger at her and cuts her off)

Bong: I'll do the talking. Number one, if you ever pull a stunt like that again, I'll consider it in my own self-defense to kill you. Nod if you understand.

(A pale-faced Moneybit frowns and nods slowly)

Bong: Now, why did you do it?

Miss Moneybit: They threatened everyone and everything I hold dear.

Bong: Why didn't you tell me or our vitamin D deficient hacker associate?

Miss Moneybit (hesitantly): I, I was afraid, I guess. Can you blame me?

Bong (sighing profoundly and staring deeply into her eyes): Well, lucky for you, I've managed to get a batch of lemonade started with the truckload of lemons you dropped on me.

Miss Moneybit (confused): Ya lost me.

Bong: I'll explain when the time is right. One more thing. Your place is bugged.

Miss Moneybit (sarcastic): Tell me something I don't know.

Bong: How'd you know?

Miss Moneybit: Come on, Bong. I've read a spy novel or two in my day.

Bong (rolling eyes): Right, silly me. Well, time's up. I gotta run.

Miss Moneybit: Wait! One more thing. You're having a huge effect, ya know. The number of people online talking about anarchy is growing exponentially. The ruling class must be hysterical right now.

Bong: Which means they're at their most dangerous, like a cornered animal. (turns around to leave)

Miss Moneybit: Feel free to knock next time.

Bong (turns around, smiling): Put your little freak-out video on Steemit and see how much you can get for it.

Miss Moneybit: Video? What video?

Scene 6

An hour after Bong's talk with Moneybit.

K is laughing his head off in front of his main computer screen.

K: Great video, Bong. Glad to see I'm not the only one you pick on.

End Episode 3

Episode 4

Scene 1

James Bong is sprawled out on the floor of K's place in Acapulco snoozing away.

K (nudging Bong with foot): Bong!

Bong (dazed): Huh, what? I'm trying to sleep.

K: You've been cuttin zees for over 12 hours, most of which has been filled with unpleasant, involuntary bodily noises.

Bong (rising to feet, sleepy-eyed, offended): Bullocks.

K: I've got holographic video to prove it if you want.

Bong (sighing): Not necessary.

K: Anyway, we've got work to do. A big job is just around the corner.

Bong: Have you managed to get some useful intel from our plants in Small's office?

K (puffy cheeks): Not exactly.

Bong: It's been a week. What the hell is taking you so long?

K: It's a lot of data to sift through! Anyway, what I do have is intel from the DEA that a big raid is about to happen in a few days.

Bong: I'm listening.

K: The biggest cannabis dispensary in California, Kushy Budz, is about to get raided.

Mysterious female voice comes from the background.

Female Voice: K, I have finished the tasks you assigned me.

Bong (turns around and is shocked to see a female humanoid robot): How long was I asleep?

Female Robot: You were sleeping for 12 hours, 9 minutes, and 3 seconds. Your snoring registered a .00000001433 on the Richter Scale. That could be a problem. Would you like a medical exam?

Bong (jaw dropped): No, I don't want a medical exam. (turns to K) What the hell have you done?

K (laughing): Bong, this is Symphy.

Bong: Where'd it come from?

K: I finished her yesterday.

Bong: You built it?
K (proudly): Yep. My finest work yet.

Bong (facepalm): OH, brother. Is that why you haven't found intel from our bugs at Small's yet?

K (twiddling thumbs nervously): Well, I'm not sure I'd say that.

Bong: In other words, a deafening yes. We need to get to Small and Sir Trax.

K: What we need, Bong, is already happening. People are learning about rights and anarchy thanks to our work. Small and Trax are just cogs, nothing more.

Bong: That might be, but I've got a personal vendetta against those cogs. Knowledge will spread, but I've got a score to settle as well with those two.

K: Yeah, I get it. That's fine. Just be patient and I'll find something we can use against them.

Bong: And in the meantime, you're building robots in your spare time.

K: She's actually a primitive form of A.I., not a robot.

Bong: Well, she's not going on any missions with me.

K: Who said she was? I wouldn't risk her to save your arrogant ass, anyway.

Bong: How comforting. So what about this raid.

K: Kushy Budz dispensary is in L.A. It's a joint raid between DEA and LAPD happening in five days.

Bong: How many agents?

K: At least 30.

Bong: That's a lot. Maybe I could use your robot's help.

K: Not a chance. I can get that number down, though.

Bong: How's that?

K: I'm gonna cancel the raid in the LAPD computer system.

Bong: Why don't you just do that to the DEA and be done with it?

K: Cuz we need more video of your daring heroics to finance our operation.

Bong: And how much did your robot cost?

K (eyes shifting): Let's stay on task, Bong.

Bong: I'm gonna need lots of toys for this one.

K: I'll have your car waiting for you in LA. It'll have everything you need in it.

Bong (skeptically): Such as?

K: A 3D printer.

Bong (gruffly): You spent all the money on your little pet robot, didn't you?

K: Well, not everything. She'll come in handy, don't you worry. You'll see!

Bong: What, scrubbing your toilets?

K: Good luck, Bong. We'll be in touch.

Bong (walking out): Don't remind me.

Scene 2

The next day, Bong walks into the colorful Kushy Budz. He wanders around and admires the plethora of artful products on display. He then approaches a chubby, pleasant-looking, narrow eyed, thickly bearded clerk.

Bong: Groovy place you've got here.

Clerk (raising eyebrow): Groovy? Um, can I help you with something?

Bong: I'm here to help, actually. What's your name?

Clerk: I'm Bush, and you are?

Bong: Bong, James Bong.

Clerk: Nice name.

Bong: Are you really named Bush?

Bush: Yep.

Bong: Your parents were…

Bush: Cruel.

Bong (pointing to another worker): If that guy's name is Clinton or Whacker, I'll have no choice but to leave.

Bush: Anyway, you said you're here to help?

Bong: You're going to be raided by the feds in 4 days.

Bush (skeptical): And how do you know that?

Bong: I'm not sure you'd believe me if I'd explain it to you.

Bush (calling to co-worker): Hey, Pigeon! Get over here!

Pigeon: I'm busy, Bush. Whatsup?

Bush: This guy says we're gonna be raided in a few days.

Pigeon looks at Bong a moment.

Pigeon: Hey, wait a minute! I've seen you before!

Bush: You have?

Pigeon: Yeah, this is that guy from those Dtube videos I was tellin you about. It's James Bong!

Bush (squinting at Bong): Great balls of fire, you're right!

Bong (confused): I told you my name up front, and who says great balls of fire?

Bush: Wait, so it's true? We're gonna be raided! Holy turkey meatball pasta!

Bong: Are you ok?

Pigeon: He's fine, he does this a lot.

Bong: Ridiculous exclamations?

Pigeon: That's his specialty. So what are you thinking about this raid?

Bong: Let's sit and have a chat and we'll go over our options.

Pigeon: Sure thing. And I'll tell ya what, we'll smoke this in your honor (holds out a huge bongload).

Bong: Actually, I don't smoke.

Pigeon and Bush look at each other in disbelief.

Bush: Were your parents major potheads or something? How did you get the name Bong, anyway?

Bong: I don't remember my parents. Anyway, my name isn't important. We've got to get busy if we want to foil this raid.

Scene 3

Bong is having a drink at a low key bar called "The Speedy Turtle".

K: Bong!

Bong looks wearily at his new smartwatch.

Bong: I've had a long day. Make it quick, K.

K: You're not gonna believe what I found.

Bong: A girlfriend?

K: Even better! I got the crew manifest for the raid and did a little digging. There's someone with very interesting connections to General Small and Sir Hugo Trax. A guy named Ty Prince.

Bong: You're joking.

K: Why is that?

Bong: We were in the same training class together.

K: I didn't see that in his profile.

Bong: That's because he failed the program.

K: I didn't know it was possible to fail the program.

Bong: Very funny. So what has Ty been up to?

K: I don't think we can get into all the details on a call like this. What I can tell you right now that is pertinent to your situation is that he works for a CIA front called Cargo Solutions.

Bong (grimacing): Damn nondescript, unimaginative naming bastards. Sorry, go ahead.

K: I couldn't agree more. Anyway, Cargo Solutions runs tons of drugs. They got in trouble with some local officials in Mexico and Columbia a few years back.

Bong: You mean they didn't pay off the right people.

K: That sounds about right, but who knows. Anyway, the whole thing blew up in their faces. Some DEA guys that aren't on the CIA dole tried to make a case against them.

Bong: Stop right there. Lemme guess, the naive DEA guys wound up having heart attacks.

K: How'd you know?

Bong: Standard procedure. So what's Prince got to do with all this?

K: He's the head of their personnel department. Look, I think that's enough info for now. The rest is really sensitive and should be discussed in person. I just thought you'd like to know before your big fireworks show.

Bong: I hate to say it, K, but you did good.

K: Actually, Symphy was a huge help. I couldn't have done it without her.

Bong (sarcastically): 3 cheers for A.I. Anything else, K?

K: Yeah, bring me back a souvenir from Kushy Budz.

Bong (rolling eyes): Goodbye, K.

End Part 1

Begin Part 2

Scene 1

The night before the raid.

Symphy: Bong, how may I assist you?

Bong (perplexed): K, did your voice change? Have you regressed to before puberty?

Symphy: This is Symphy. Would you like to speak to K?

Bong: Immediately.

K: Hey Bong! What a pleasant surprise!

Bong (gruff): So now it's your secretary. How quaint.

K: You're just jealous. Tomorrow's the big day. Whatsup?

Bong: I need one of those clear skin trackers.

K: So print one.

Bong: Do you think I'd be calling you if I could print one?

K: Just use the 3D printer. Are you that helpless?

Bong: There's no schematic for it, you arrogant little twerp.

K (flustered): Oh, right. Sorry about that. I'll wire it to the printer now. What's it for?

Bong: You'll find out soon enough. (taps smartwatch to end call)

Scene 2

Bong is having one final meeting with the staff of Kushy Budz Dispensary before the expected raid by the DEA.

Bong: Ok, one more time over the checklist before I head out. Gasmasks.

Pigeon: Check.

Bong: Enough aerosolized THC to knock out a fleet of stallions.

Bush: Double check.

Bong: Rope and tape?
Pigeon: Check and check. What about guns?

Bong: Well, I've got one. It's your property. I'd hope you'd have guns to protect it.

Bush (uncertain): Um, well, I think Pigeon has a pistol.

Pigeon: Yeah, I've got a pistol.

Bong (amazed): You've got to be kidding! You expect to hold off a DEA raid with one pistol?

Bush: Hey, you're the one who dreamed up our whole defense. After all, if the plan works, we shouldn't need the guns, right?

Bong (grimacing): Let's hope the plan works. Ok, I'm going to keep watch from my car. Remember, I'll call you when they're approaching. You won't have much time, so be ready.

Bong walks out and goes across the street to his 3D printed black car modeled after the 1977 Trans Am. After waiting for 30 minutes, Bong sees a train of black SUVs and Chargers cruising towards him at a feverish pace. Bong dials Bush's number.

Bong (beeping sound from smartwatch): Come on, come on, pick up.

Bush is smoking a bongload, watching a holographic Dtube video of epic fails, and laughing his chubby ass off.

20 seconds go by…..no answer.

Bong (in anguish): That cheeky little (incoherent growling)

Bong runs into the dispensary just as the black motorcade pulls up outside.

Bong: They're here! They're here! Masks on!

All the workers throw their masks on and hide behind various pieces of furniture. Bong heads upstairs and squats down behind a statue of a stoned frog, where he has a sniper's view of the bottom floor.

The doors burst open and 13 black clad thugs in DEA uniforms and heavy gear come in with firearms pointing all around.

Ty Prince: This is a raid! Everyone hands up now!

Bush hits the red button on a computer joystick, which releases highly concentrated, aerosolized THC into the air. The gas knocks out all the would-be raiders.

Bong runs down and takes a look outside to make sure there aren't any stragglers.

Bong (muffled from the gas mask): Great job, everyone! Ok, time for the tape and rope.

Pigeon (muffled): What? You're muffled because of the mask.

Bong: What?
Pigeon: What?

Bong (grabs tape and rope off glass display case, then yells): Rope and tape!

In a few minutes, all of the would-be raiders are bound up, the air clears, and everyone takes their masks off. Bong takes the opportunity to slap the clear skin tracker on the back of Prince's neck.

Pigeon: So what now?

Bong: When they wake up, we'll make them an offer. They can leave on their own volition after promising to never violate private property again. If they refuse, we knock them out again and leave them somewhere.

30 minutes later.

Prince (weary eyed): What the?

Bong: Attention everyone! We've got a talker!

Prince: Bong? I thought you were dead.
Bong: Now why would you think a silly thing like that?

Prince: Because (hesitates) Well, I have my sources.

Bong (laughing); A source of BS. So here's the deal. You and your thugs here can leave, peacefully, on your own accord, after you promise no more private property violations.

Prince (cocky): Dream on, Bong.

Bong: Or we can just knock you out again and leave you stranded somewhere. I hear Death Valley is wonderful this time of year.

The rest of the DEA cowards begin to come to.

Thug 1: What happened, boss?

Prince: An old friend has made his presence known.

Bong: So what's it gonna be, Prince?

Pigeon (standing over Prince with his little pistol, trying to act tough): Yeah, what's it gonna be, Prince? (pauses) Hey, wait a minute. How do you know this guy's name?

Bong: Long story.

Prince: Ok, Bong. We'll go. But now you're on my radar.

Bong (sarcastically): Looks like I'm already six feet under, then. Say hi to your "sources" for me. (turns to Bush) We can start untying them. Be ready to hit the button in case they try anything funny. (turns to Prince) You'll be allowed to leave, one by one.

Scene 3

2 days later, Bong is sitting at a poker table in Las Vegas.

K: Bong!

Bong: K, as usual, your timing is abysmal. I'm on an extremely hot streak right now.

K: Just wanted to let you know that the Kushy Budz video has gone viral on Dtube. We're looking at a fat payday! Don't blow it at the casino.

Bong (smiling): And don't blow yours on anymore frankenstein robots.

K: So what's next?

Bong: Now we wait for Prince to pop up somewhere that can be used to our advantage. This is going to be epic.

End Episode 4

Episode 5

Scene 1 – K is passed out with his face planted in a keyboard. His humanoid robot Symphy is playing 3D chess with itself. A call comes in on one of the many computers strewn about the hacker lair. Symphy answers.

Symphy: Hello, how may I assist you?

Miss Moneybit (confused and astonished): Umm, do I have the right number? Where's K?

Symphy (robotic laugh): Oh, yes, you have not made an error. Don't worry. Master K is passed out on a keyboard right now. May I take a message?

Miss Moneybit: Um, who are you?

36

Symphy: I am Master K's humanoid assistant and companion.

Miss Moneybit: I guess the dude finally gave up on real women. Why do I find relief in that? (pauses to ponder) Anyway, wake him up. It's important.

Symphy: I'm afraid that goes against my behavior protocols. Please give me your name and I'll relay a message.

Miss Moneybit (sighing): I'm Miss Moneybit. Trust me, he's gonna wanna see me.

Symphy: Oh! You're Miss Moneybit? Yes, you are one of the only exceptions to his sleeping rule. I'll wake him at once.

Symphy walks over to K and slaps him on the back of the head.

Miss Moneybit: Not too subtle. I like your style.

K awakens with a start and blurts out….

K: No, I swear, they're not mine!

Miss Moneybit's holographic image appears in the room next to K.

Miss Moneybit: What aren't yours?

K (looking Miss Moneybit up and down): Oh, good morning!

Symphy: It is two in the afternoon.

K: Did you just call to say you love me?

Miss Moneybit: Your sense of humor is impeccable. No, but I do have news that'll peak your interest. Go to my Steemit feed.

K (looking at a bigscreen monitor on the wall): You have a viral anti-TSA video. You flew old commercial? What the hell were you thinking? Why didn't you just fly SteemAir or something?

Miss Moneybit (pouty): It's a long story. I'd rather not talk about it. Anyway, so those goons in costumes, ya know the so-called TSA agents, wouldn't let half my stuff go on my flight with me. They frisked me….twice. I was damn near crying. Me! Can you believe that?

K: You are one tough cookie, I'll give ya that. At least you got it all on tape.

Miss Moneybit: I was thinking revenge, with a twist.

K: Hell hath no fury like a woman scorned.

Symphy: This expression puzzles me.

K; Don't fry your circuits over it.

Miss Moneybit: Wanna hear my plan?

K (cheesy grin and voice): I'm always interested in more time with you.

Miss Moneybit: I know. It was more of a rhetorical question. So I wanna get a big group of people together to walk through a TSA rights destruction chokepoint. No IDs, no searches, total freedom. Just a giant throng of people marching past those order following bastards!

K: Wow, you're really fired up! I like it! And I like the plan. How are you gonna draw the crowd?

Miss Moneybit: I figure profit sharing will be the easiest and fastest way. I'll offer a percentage of the video I shoot of the whole thing. I'll keep it to a hundred people or less. Enough to be effective, but not too many to dilute the monetary pool. What do ya think?

K: Genius. You should have everyone carry a big bottle of water, too. Where do I come in?

Miss Moneybit: You don't. I could use Bong's help, though. Where's he at?

K: Beats me. And I'm not so sure he's too anxious to see you.

Miss Moneybit (offended): Why do you say that?

K: Well, you did put a tracker on him a few weeks ago, remember?

Miss Moneybit: But we kissed and made up.

K: In your dreams.

Symphy (perplexed): Miss Moneybit, do you find James Bong attractive?

Miss Moneybit: Yeah, me and a million other women.

Symphy: I don't understand why.

Miss Moneybit: K, did you program her to find twerps like you attractive?

K: We're getting off track here. I'll try and track down Bong and see if he'll help your TSA bit. When's your target date?
Miss Moneybit: 3 days. When word gets out, I don't want to give the feds any time to subvert it.

K: Smart.

Miss Moneybit: I'll keep you posted.

K: You don't want to stay and watch me drink coffee?

Symphy: Human behavior puzzles me greatly.

Scene 2

James Bong is sitting at a secluded bar called the Tipsy Camel.

Bong (staring at his near finished drink): Do you ever do things you don't want to do, but feel that you have to?

Bartender: Every time I wake up in the morning I have a similar feeling.

Bong (smirking, polishes off the rest of his drink in a giant swig): Well, this is one of those moments for me.

Bartender: More important than drinking?

Bong: Afraid so. I've got a call to make.

Bong throws money on the bar and walks off. He gets out his new blockchain encrypted smartwatch and calls K. Symphy answers the call.

Symphy: Hello, who's calling?

Bong: Bong, James Bong.

Symphy: Would you like to speak with Master K?

Bong: I unfortunately have to speak with K and I highly recommend that you don't inflate his ego by calling him master.

K: Bong! Your timing is impeccable, aside from the fact that you interrupted a record setting Tetris game I was in.

Bong: How's that?

K proceeds to tell Bong about Miss Moneybit's plan.

Bong: I'm not going anywhere near the DC airport, and certainly not for her. I still don't trust her.

K: Look, Bong, I don't blame you for that. I don't trust her a hundred percent either. However, take into account that if the feds send in agent provocateurs to muddle things up, it could cause some serious problems for Moneybit.

Bong (huffing): I see your point.
K: Maybe don't get involved directly. She doesn't even have to know that you're going. Just keep an eye out for feds and make sure Moneybit stays safe.

Bong: Ok, ok, I'll do it. Now what about Prince? He hasn't popped up in any places of interest since the dispensary affair?

K: Nope, not yet. I've got Symphy tracking him, so we won't miss a beat.

Bong: So when is the big day in DC?

K: 3 days, high noon.

Bong: Sounds melodramatic. Anything else?

K: Yeah, keep your smartwatch on so I can reach you.

Bong: I'll do it on one condition. Symphy doesn't call you master anymore.

K: I'm hanging up now.

Scene 3

2 days later in The City of London, Sir Hugo Trax is having a meeting with an old, shadowy character in a limo.

Trax: I can assure you, sir, I'll be personally handling the selection this time. I won't disappoint you.

Old Shadowy Character: You know how my milieu and I hate to be disappointed.

Trax (nervously): Oh, yes sir, I remember very well what happened to the last wretched soul that failed you.

Old Shadowy Character (smug): Very well. You go tomorrow, is that right?

Trax: Yes, I'll be on my way to L.A. first thing in the morning.

Old Shadowy Character (ominous tone): You know how I hate rhymes.

Trax: Sorry, sir, not sure what came over me.

Old Shadowy Character (sighing deeply): Very well, now be on your way.

Trax (grimacing): Sir, I believe the car is moving. Perhaps I'll get out at the next stop.

Old Shadowy Character: Next stop? This isn't a bloody bus, now is it? Out you go now. No whining.

Trax (gulps heavily): Of course, sir. (Jumps out of the limo and rolls on the pavement. Bystanders scream. Trax covers his face and runs away.)

End Part 1
Begin Part 2

Scene 1

Bong is driving his 3D printed 1977 Black Trans Am en route to Dulles Airport in the DC area. He's having a chat with K before attending Miss Moneybit's big TSA confrontation event.

Bong: Moneybit doesn't know I'm coming, right?

K: Of course not. You know how well I keep secrets.

Bong: Which is why I asked again.

K: More importantly, we finally got a lead on Prince.

Bong: About time you delivered.

K: And not just Prince, either. It appears that we have an ominous continuity.

Bong: Explain.

K: So I intercepted a message from the bug in General Small's office. Looks like Hugo Trax is going to L.A. today. And guess who showed up in L.A. yesterday? Ty Prince. How about that?

Bong: Looks like I need to get going quick then.

K: You gotta watch Moneybit's back first, though, ok?

Bong (reluctantly): I suppose. I'm at the airport. Gotta go.

Bong puts his iris-changing contacts on so the iris scanners won't recognize him. He quickly makes his way to the designated checkpoint where Moneybit's show is about to begin. While waiting near the checkpoint, he spots a throng of at least 100 people walking confidently towards the area. Leading the pack is Miss Moneybit. Bong eyes the 6 TSA order-following dupes, who have no idea what they're in for. Moneybit and another 10 people walk in lockstep at the front as the TSA goons try to stop them and ask for ID and tickets. The goons are ignored and are quickly passed by. After a moment, one of the goons panics and tries to grab one of the free humans.

TSA goon: Stop, stop! I command you to stop!

Everyone ignores the goon and continues to walk through the feeble checkpoint. Suddenly, 4 individuals wearing black hoodies in the middle of the pack start throwing rocks at the TSA agents. Chaos ensues.

Bong (to himself): Agent provocateurs!

The TSA goons start cowering behind the naked body scanners and start calling for police intervention on their radios.

Bong runs into the pack and knocks out two of the black block provocateurs with one thunderous roundhouse. He then kicks another one in the testicles, and drops the fourth and final one with a knee to the skull. A handful of badge-wearing, order-following parasites in blue start running to the scene. The protesters continue to march through the checkpoint undeterred. Bong spots Moneybit, who is panic stricken and confused just past the checkpoint. Bong bursts through the chaotic mess of bodies, grabs Moneybit by the arm, and the two sprint away from the area. One police goon chases them, but fails to reach them before Bong and Moneybit are safely cruising away in Bong's Trans Am.

Moneybit (shrieking): What the hell are you doing?

Bong: Saving your arse. Thanks for the gratitude.

Moneybit: What?

Bong: Don't you get it? Did you forget that you're being watched by Small and Trax? They've been waiting for you to screw up, and now you've done those tools a favor.

Moneybit: What the hell happened back there?

Bong: Agent provocateurs attacking the TSA goons, that's what. And now they're gonna put out a narrative that you led a violent revolt against the TSA. I knew this was a bad idea.

Moneybit: Where are we going?

Bong (wryly): I'm gonna put you on a plane to your destination of choice. Might I suggest Acapulco? I know a pasty little nerd that'll wet his pants if you do.

Moneybit (incredulous): You've got to be kidding! I'm going home!

Bong: There are at least a dozen order-following little dogs at your house right now, guaranteed, just waiting to throw you in a cage.

Moneybit: I can't just leave the country.

Bong: I can't afford to lose you.

Moneybit (gushy and googly eyed): Awww, that's so sweet.

Bong: You're too valuable of an asset.

Moneybit (huffy, sarcastic): You're so sentimental.

Bong: Take a picture of my eyes.

Moneybit: What? Why?

Bong: I got the iris prints of the agent provocateurs stored in my contacts. Get the prints to K. It might be useful to identify them. (Bong hands a smartphone to Moneybit) Here, take this and get a private flight to Acapulco booked ASAP. Use Swarm City so it can be anonymous. I've gotta get to L.A.

Moneybit: L.A.? What's going on, Bong?

Bong (smirking gruffly): Ominous continuity. Get ready for a big story.
An hour later, Bong drops Moneybit at a private airfield in rural Virginia for her flight to Acapulco.

Moneybit: This is crazy.

Bong: Welcome to my life. Tell your boyfriend I said hello.

Moneybit: I hate you, Bong.

Moneybit boards the plane and takes off. Bong proceeds to a different airfield to pick up a private plane and fly himself to L.A.

Scene 2

Now after sunset, James Bong is walking from his private plane to his new 3D printed midnight blue car modeled after the 1986 Ferrari Testarossa. He calls K.

Bong: Ok, K, where's Prince at? Being in L.A. makes me nauseous due to its overt oozing of evil.

K: What I'm about to tell you isn't going to help your severe allergy to evil.

Bong (takes deep breath): Lay it on me. I'm ready.

K: Ty Prince is in Beverly Hills.

Bong: Beverly Hills is fairly large. Do you think we can narrow that down a bit?

K: You didn't let me finish. He's at Kevin Spacey's house.

Bong: Bullocks.

K: Not joking. You have your cameras ready?

Bong: One on each shoulder.

K: Can you get an autograph for me?

Bong (gruff): I'm replacing you as soon as possible. (click)

Scene 3

Bong is squatting behind some obelisk-shaped hedges in Kevin Spacey's yard. He watches through a window by zooming in with his special iris-scanning contacts. He sees Ty Prince, Kevin Spacey, Harvey Weinstein, and Sir Hugo Trax drinking cocktails and lounging in overstuffed leather thrones.

Prince: Hugo, you get first pick.

Spacey: You G-men always stick together, don't you. Why can't I have first pick for once?

Weinstein: We could draw straws or something.

Trax: Or maybe Kev would prefer a sword-fighting tournament?
Spacey: Low blow, even for you, Trax.

Prince nods to a bulky order-follower in a black suit. The order-follower opens the door next to him, goes downstairs, and returns a moment later with a 12-year-old girl.

Trax (waving her away): No, no, not a chance. Look at that blemish on her cheek. Not a chance, no.

Spacey: Old Harv will take her. He takes anything with a pulse.

Trax: Can't we just go and have a look at all of them together? I mean, really. This isn't a damned pageant.

All keep silent and raise eyebrows.

Trax: Great, then. It's settled.

Spacey: To the magic dungeon!

All four stand up and start to walk downstairs. Bong takes the opportunity to enter the house. He stealthily gets to the top of the stairs and has a birds-eye view of the group. He is appalled by the scene. There are at least 20 drugged-up, naked girls in cages between the ages of 10 and 16.

Trax: Prince, my boy, you've outdone yourself this time.

Prince: I thought it was a good haul.

Spacey: Can we sample before we buy?

Prince: You know the rules.

Trax (pointing): That dark skinned one there, where is she from?

Prince: Venezuela.

Trax: And the blond with the icy blue eyes?

Prince: Russia.

Trax: Saved from war torn areas, what a hero you are, Prince. Those two will do nicely. What about the youngest ones? Where are they from?

Prince: US of A. Homegrown talent.

Weinstein: They can understand what we're saying? You fool!

Trax: Calm down. They'll just have to be eliminated after they serve their purpose. But you really shouldn't get English speakers, you know. It's an unnecessary risk.

Prince (shrugging shoulders): My contact at CPS gave me an offer I couldn't refuse.

Trax: How much for the four, then?
Prince: 20 million.

Trax: The money and transport will be here in an hour.

Weinstein: Leaving so soon?

Trax: I have a real job, unlike you.

Bong pulls out some canisters of aerosolized THC, opens them, and holds the door shut.

Spacey (alarmed): You boys here something?

The gas spreads quickly and soon all in the dungeon are knocked out. After waiting a few minutes for the air to clear, Bong hurries downstairs and ties up the criminals. He then uses his smart devices. He uses the Sub-Stratum network, SteemPay, and Swarm City to arrange drone delivery of clothing for the girls to Spacey's house. He also arranges a transport bus and a cargo plane. The clothing arrives in less than an hour, just as everyone starts to wake from the THC-induced slumber. Bong starts handing clothes out to the girls, most of whom are too scared to speak. The criminals also awaken but cannot speak because their mouths are taped up.

Trax (muffled, trying to yell at Bong): Bmmmmph!

Bong: Hell, Mr. Trax. You said that the 20 million will be arriving soon? What should I do with it? Should I burn it? Should I allow the girls to take it? Comments? (Bong laughs to himself at Trax's inability to speak)

Bong: Tell me, Trax, do you know the difference between right and wrong? No, I know you don't. Why? Number one, because of your actions. And number two, because you're an evil statist tool.

Bong checks his smartwatch and runs up the stairs, then outside to see what vehicles have arrived. A limo is pulling slowly up the driveway. Bong waits out of sight, then pounces on the driver. He knocks out the driver with a left hook and grabs the briefcase of cash next to the driver. The transport van that Bong ordered pulls up moments later. Bong runs back to the dungeon.

Bong: Girls, you can fly with me to safety, or you can stay here with these criminals. The choice is yours. The girls follow Bong. They drive to a private airfield outside the city where the cargo plane is waiting. Bong flies through the night and arrives in Acapulco at dawn.

Bong: This is where we part ways, girls. You're free. Divide the money and start a new life, if you wish.

The oldest girl, all of 16, speaks up.

Girl: That's it? You're leaving us?

Bong (uncertain what to do): Well, I can't take care of you.

Girl: What are we supposed to do?

Bong (reluctantly): I suppose you can come with me and we'll figure something out.

20 minutes later at K's place, Miss Moneybit and K are chatting in K's living room/hacker lair.

Miss Moneybit: Do you hear something?

Bong is outside picking the lock.

Symphy: There is an intruder at the door.

K: Bong!

K runs to the door to surprise Bong.

K: Surprise!

Bong: What the hell?

K (smug): You can't get past Symphy. Besides, can't you just knock?

Bong: Old habits die hard. We've got visitors.

K looks in the background and sees the large group of young girls.

K: Looks like you've got one hell of a story.

Bong: That's just getting started.

End Episode 5

Episode 6

Scene 1

City of London, England

Sir Hugo Trax is riding in the back of a stretch limo with an old, shadowy character.

Shadowy Character: Bong?

Trax: Yes, sir. James Bong, a former MI6 agent.

Shadowy Character: He's the reason that I have to tell my associates that we don't have the necessary goods for our little party?

Trax: I'm afraid so.

Shadowy Character: Oh, dear. Do you know how much my associates and I hate to be let down like this?

Trax: I can only imagine, sir. I might as well go ahead and tell you another bit from my trip to LA.

Shadowy Character: I'm listening impatiently.

Trax: Bong has been working with a blogger who has quite the following. He filmed the whole charade and it's gone viral online.

Shadowy Character squeezes champagne goblet in his hand until it shatters.

Trax: On the bright side, we are actively discrediting the blogger in all major news outlets to minimize the damage.

Shadowy Character: What shall we do with Mr. Bong then?

Trax: Whatever you feel is best.

Shadowy Character: Please stop groveling. It's too late to save face for you. I want you to bring Bong to me.

Trax: I feel it would be easier to just kill him, sir.

Shadowy Character: Your feelings are not a factor in this equation, Mr. Trax. You will bring me Bong or every descendant of yours will suffer the most unimaginable sufferings. How do you feel now, Mr. Trax?

Trax: Quite motivated. You will have Bong, Mr. Gateschild.

Gateschild: Much better, Trax, that's a good boy. Now you may leave.

Trax: We're still moving quite fast, sir.

Gateschild: Yes, I recommend you roll. Jumping out of cars at high speed can be quite hazardous.

Trax jumps out of the limo and Gateschild smirks with pleasure.

Scene 2

K's house in Acapulco, Mexico.

K, Bong, and Miss Moneybit are drinking coffee at a cluttered dining room table. K's female humanoid robot Symphy is standing nearby.

Miss Moneybit: Your place is such a pigsty.

K stuffs donuts into his mouth and chews deliberately with mouth open.

Miss Moneybit: So gross.

K continues his overly-zealous enjoyment.

Miss Moneybit: How can someone who eats like you weigh like 90 pounds?

K: Bong, can you take her back to DC?

Bong (mildly amused): You're tired of her already? Ever hear the expression, be careful what you wish for, you just might get it?

Miss Moneybit: Can't your robot do some cleaning? She's just standing there.

K: She's far too advanced to relegate herself to housework.

Miss Moneybit (rolling eyes): Whatever.

Bong: So Moneybit, all the girls are doing well?

Moneybit (peppy): Yep! They're sharing 3 houses in the same neighborhood. I've started them on the trivium and some of them have business ideas they already want to pursue.

Bong (pleased look): That's great to hear. I'm very happy for them.

Moneybit: Oh, James, you're such a big softy! (rubs Bong on the back)

K (jealous): Hey, I helped too!

Moneybit: That's nice.

K: So I see your Steemit blog is blowing up. Over a million views on Dtube for the rescue video! You can go ahead and cut me my share of the payout.

Moneybit: Very funny.

Bong: I don't want to rain on anyone's parade, but I'm sure you've seen in the lamestream media that they're trying to discredit you, Moneybit. They're saying that the violence at your TSA protest was your fault, and that you're a "violent anarchist".

Moneybit: Quite ironic coming from violent statists.

K: I'm not too worried about it. The more the lamestream media like BNN try to discredit someone, the more popular they become. Isn't that right, Symphy?

Symphy: Master K is correct. When the largest 100 news outlets attempt to paint someone in a bad light, nearly 70 percent of the time the individual becomes more well-known and popular. I have a question. What is BNN?

K: The Bullshit News Network.

Symphy (head tilted sideways, confused): I am not aware of any such network.

K (laughing): It's what we call CNN. It's a joke, Symphy.

Symphy (still perplexed): I find humor difficult.

K: You're less than a month old. You'll learn.

Symphy: Master K, why have you not told Bong about your nephew?

K: I was waiting for the right moment.

Bong (surprised): Nephew? I didn't even know you had any siblings.

K: Yeah, an older sister. We don't talk much. She's a statist, so it's hard.

Bong: So whatsup with your nephew?

K: Ok, so my nephew, Caesar, is five. My sister, Helen, has refused to vaccinate him before he starts school.

Moneybit: You mean authoritarian indoctrination camp. Why doesn't she just home educate?

K: Remember, she's a statist. She thinks extortion funded prisons for children are great.

Moneybit: But she knows vaccines are bad?

K: Yeah, she's not completely brainwashed. Anyway, the school reported it to CPS, so now CPS is trying to steal my nephew from my sister.

Moneybit: Oh my God! (turns to Bong) James,

Bong cuts her off…

Bong: Say no more. I'll be happy to help, and even happier to crush those dirty CPS parasites.

Moneybit: And a bit curious to meet K's family, I imagine.

Bong: I must admit I'm a tad curious. This should make for quite the Dtube video.

49

K: Please, no filming!

Moneybit: Are you ashamed of your sister?

K: Ashamed is such a strong word.

Bong: Where do they live?

K: Vegas.

Moneybit: Vegas, baby! Can I come?

Bong: Not a chance.

Scene 3

James Bong is approaching the affluent looking house of K's sister Helen in Las Vegas.

Bong (thinking to himself): Wow, looks like K's sister does well for herself financially. I certainly wasn't expecting this.

Bong rings the doorbell and loathes the heat while he's waiting. A breathtakingly-beautiful twenty-something year old blond woman answers the door.

Blond: Can I help you?

Bong (looking around, confused): I'm sorry, I must be in the wrong place. I'm looking for Helen.

Blond: And who may I ask are you?

Bong: Bong, James Bong.

Helen: (sighing deeply): My brother sent you.

Bong: Correct.

Helen: Why did you think you were at the wrong house?

Bong (thinking of K's scrawny and unkept physical features, then looks at K's gorgeous sister): Oh, no reason. Maybe the heat. Not sure.

Helen: Would you like to come in?

Bong: Yes, perhaps we could speak in private.

They enter the spotless, shiny, well organized home of Helen.

Bong (jaw dropping open): Are you sure K is your brother?

Helen (giggling): Yes! Why?

Bong: Forget it. I think you might know why K sent me here.

Helen (on the verge of tears): They're gonna take my baby boy.

Bong: I won't let that happen.

Helen: I appreciate your offer to help, but (pauses out of discomfort)

Bong: You have reservations about me helping you. Why?

Helen: Two things, I guess. Even if you stop them this time, they'll just keep coming back, won't they?

Bong: That might be true. You'll need to defend yourself and your rights, for sure. Let me ask you this. Isn't it better to die for liberty, than to live as a slave?

Helen: That might be true, Mr. Bong. But another thing is

Bong: You don't want our help because we're anarchists.

Helen (nodding yes): It's just that I know you guys usually make video and put it online.

Bong: And you don't want to be associated with us.

Helen sobs and nods yes.

Bong: Look, if you don't want my help, just say the word, and I'll be on my way.

Helen: Maybe we can compromise.

Bong: How's that?

Helen: You don't record.

Bong: We finance our operations with the money made on our videos. You don't think we fly all over the world and have tons of high-tech gadgets without financing, do you? Freedom is becoming quite popular these days. I think I have a solution, though. I'll help remotely.

Helen: You can do that?

Bong (smirking): Yeah, you'll see.

Helen: I don't know when they're gonna show up, though.
Bong: K and I will know ahead of time. We'll give you ample warning. Do you have any guns?

Helen (reluctantly): Just a revolver.

Bong: Hopefully you won't need it, but it's good to know you have it. Well, I best be going now. We'll be in touch.

Helen shows Bong out.

Helen: Say hi to my brother for me.

Bong: You should do it yourself.

Scene 4

Bong is sitting at a blackjack table at Caesar's Palace. K's voice startles Bong.

K: Bong!

Bong: For once, your timing is actually good. I'm getting killed.

K: Epic news. Need some privacy.

Bong (as he walks away from the table): A blackjack table isn't private enough?

K: Call me back.

Bong goes out a back way and ends up by a dumpster.

Bong: Ok, K, make it quick. This smell isn't mixing well with my martini.

K: 2 things. I intercepted a CPS communique. They'll be at my sister's tomorrow at 9am.

Bong: Looks like I'll need a few more martinis to make sure I'm up early.

K: Very funny. Now get this. Symphy has been scanning through all the data from General Small's office. She also dug deep into the paper trail of the CIA front company Ty Prince runs drugs for, Cargo Solutions, remember?

Bong: With a catchy name like that, how could I forget?

K: Symphy went through like a zillion shell companies and found the majority stakeholder in Cargo Solutions. Any guesses?

Bong: Hmmm, a bankster?

K: Of course. More specifically, Machiavelli Enterprises. And you know who owns them?

Bong: Machiavelli Bank, of course.

K: Yep. And that bank has ties to all sorts of old money oligarchs, aristocrats, royal families. You name it. It's the whose who of the ruling class. Hell, that bank is so important, they even put one of their own in as president. Philip Gateschild himself.

Bong: This is getting very interesting.

K: This is getting very dangerous.

Bong: Just the way I like it. One more thing before I go.

K: What's that?

Bong: Are you adopted?

End Episode 6

Episode 7

Scene 1

James Bong is at a house in Vegas that he rented on Steem BnB from a fellow voluntarist. He's got multiple smart devices scattered around the living room, which Bong has turned into a makeshift command center. He gets a call from K on his smartwatch.

K: Bong!

Bong: I'm busy.

K: I know, that's one reason I called.

Bong: You're a disturbed little man. You know that, right?

A hologram of K pops up in the room.

K: That's what all the ladies say. Anyway, how do you like the design of the new drones?

Bong: A drone that looks like a flying bong. Quite innovative. I'm sure they'll be a big hit. Pun not intended.

K: Not only that, but they're hemp-powered, too!

Bong glances at a live video feed near K's sister's house. He sees one government vehicle and a police car approaching.

Bong: Looks like its showtime. Hopefully your drones are effective, and not just fancy techno-eye-candy.

K (brashly): I'll stay on the line in case you need my expert assistance.

A jarhead-looking male cop, a toupee-toting CPS worker, and a plump female CPS worker with lobster eyes approach the home of Helen and knock. Helen answers.

Helen (nervously): Hello.

Toupee-toter: Good morning. We're with the CPS. This is concerning your son, Caesar. May we come in?

Helen (gulps, flushes red): No, you can't. This is private property. I'd appreciate it if you'd leave, all three of you, and never return.

Cop steps to the front of the group and intervenes.

Cop: Miss, I'll have to insist we're allowed to enter. We have a court order that your son is to be taken into state custody.

54

Suddenly, a loud buzzing noise interrupts the confrontation. Everyone looks up and sees 4 drones hovering, one on each side of the house.

Toupee-toter: Are those drones?

Cop: Nothing gets past you! Hmmm, something strange about their shape. They look like bongs.

Lobster Eyes: Now I've seen it all.

Bong's voice comes down from one of the drones.

Bong: You are trespassing on private property. Please leave peacefully, or you will be forcefully removed.

Lobster Eyes: We're not leaving here without the little boy!

Bong: I have four armed drones which beg to differ. Please leave peacefully. Helen and Caesar have done nothing wrong. You, agents of the state, are funded by theft and are now trying to steal a child through violent coercion.

Toupee-toter (turns to cop): Well, aren't you gonna do something?

Cop: I'm outgunned four to one. What can I do?

Lobster Eyes (huffy): How brave.

Cop: Hey lady, I didn't take this job cuz I'm brave. I took it for the pension.

Toupee-toter (turns to Helen): You haven't heard the last of us.

The three get in their extortion-funded vehicles and speed away. Helen waves to one of the drones.

Helen (crying): Thanks, Bong! Thanks, K!

Scene 2

General Small is in his office, having a phone conversation with Sir Hugo Trax.

Trax: Somehow, general, Bong is always one step ahead of us, almost as if he knows what we're doing.

General Small: Hey, don't try and pin what happened to you in L.A. on me.

Trax: Look, all I know is, he's getting intel somehow. Either you're leaking, or he's got to have a bug planted somewhere. My boss is breathing down my neck, and we work in a hierarchy, you know, so now I've got to breathe down your neck. That's how these things work!

General Small: I'll have my office swept for bugs, right away, sir.

Trax: One more thing before I go. You realize, of course, that if you don't find any bugs, then I'll have no choice but to think that you're a leak. You'd then have to be eliminated. Nothing personal, of course.

General Small: Don't worry, sir. I know it's not personal.

Trax ends call.

A chubby man with a smooshy face and a receding hairline comes to the entrance of Small's office.

Small: Do I know you?

Man: No, you don't. I work in the Total Information Awareness Office.

Small (curt voice): I see. Well, if you have total information awareness, then you must know what I'm thinking.

Man: Not really, but I did overhear part of your conversation with Trax.

Small (outraged): So you're the leak!

Man: You had the door open. What was I supposed to do, cover my ears?

Small (rushed): So what brings you here. I'm a very busy man.

Man: Some alarming information has come to my attention. Shall I close the door?

Small: No, I like it open for ventilation. Go on.

Man: As you wish. I noticed a trend in domestic, as well as global, communications recently. It seems that in the past 3 months, the number of positive mentions of keywords like "anarchy" and "anarchism" have gone up by over 3,000 percent. Not only that, but the number of people searching for the meaning of the word "anarchy" has had a similar upsurge.

Small: You mean people are actually looking up the meaning of words?

Man (sad tone): I'm afraid so, sir.

Small: Well, 3,000 percent doesn't seem so bad. What does that make, like 3,000 people?

Man: Actually, we estimate in the tens of thousands, possibly pushing six figures.

Small: Oh, that's not too many. Let me know when it gets into the millions.

Man: Don't you think we should nip this in the bud, sir, before it escalates, rather than later?

Small: I believe you're being a bit paranoid.

Man: I'm just saying that if Bong continues his exploits, then these numbers are sure to increase.

Small (red-faced): Ah ha! So you're a Bong sympathizer!?

Man: If I were a Bong sympathizer, then why would I be giving you this information right now?

Small: Hmmm, good point. I'm gonna keep an eye on you, though.

Man (walking off): Whatever.

Scene 3

Philip Gateschild is at a mansion in the English countryside. He's speaking with an old, nefarious character.

Philip: It appears that your past sexual exploits are coming back to haunt us.

Nefarious Character: Wouldn't be the first time.

Philip: A certain James Bong has been causing problems for our dogs all over America, but one of his most recent exploits had a direct effect on us, I'm afraid. He stopped the procurement of some necessary sacrifices, and now there are many in our milieu who are quite unhappy.

Nefarious Character (shocked): That can't be! I was assured when I gave him up and approved the program, that it would be fool-proof. Does anyone know he's my child?

Philip: I don't believe anyone knows, except for the ones involved in his program. Apparently, scientific methods don't always have the outcome we expect. Even the most perfect methods of control sometimes fail when confronted with the human spirit.

Nefarious Character: So what shall we do to remedy this?

Philip: I've already ordered him to be brought to me. I want you to tell him about his past. Perhaps we can neutralize him somehow. Give him a boatload of money to keep his mouth shut and disappear.

Nefarious Character: And if that doesn't work?

Philip: I'll shoot him. Nothing personal, of course.

Nefarious Character: Agreed. Make it happen, Philip. We must clear this up at once.

End Episode 7

57

Episode 8

Scene 1

K is dancing to Michael Jackson's "Billy Jean". He's wearing a Star Wars t-shirt, tight high-water jeans, and a fedora. He thinks he's alone…..

Miss Moneybit (giggling): Hey K.

K (shocked, gasps): Hey, how'd you get in here?!

Miss Moneybit: Symphy let me in.

K (turning to Symphy): You're not programmed to let people in without my authorization!

Symphy: Miss Moneybit made a very convincing argument which overrode my programming.

K (arms folded): Do tell.

Symphy (innocent smile): She said that allowing her to see you dance would be a great lesson in humor for me and that any improvement to myself would ultimately benefit you.

K: Interesting logic.

Moneybit (still giggling): I haven't told you the best part! I'm filming this!

K: Not funny.

Moneybit: Not a joke. This should earn a handsome profit on Dtube.

K: Where's the camera?

Moneybit: Hidden on me. And no, you're not allowed to look for it.

K (whiny): You're not really posting it on Dtube, are you?

Moneybit: Oh, relax. No, I'm not.

K (relieved): Whew, thanks.

Moneybit (satisfied grin, ear to ear): I'll just save it for a special time when I need to blackmail you.

K (sighing): So what brings you by?

Moneybit: I'm bored and my Spanish isn't so good, so my options are limited.

58

K: Your brutal honesty is appreciated.

Moneybit: And I've had a bit of tequila, too. Where's Bong?

K: Getting away from it all.
Moneybit: Even you?

K: Especially me.

Moneybit: Do you have any idea where he goes?

K: Nope. That's how he is. Enigmatic to the core.

Moneybit: And he has no family?

K: So he says. Anytime the subject is broached, he gets edgy.

Symphy: K, I'm sorry to interrupt, but there is breaking news regarding altcoins that I think you'll find pertinent.

K: Thanks, Symphy. Throw it on the holoscreen.

A hologram of a news broadcast coming from the BBC pops up in the middle of K's living room.

K: Wow, Symphy, you were right. This is big. The English government is putting a 20 percent tax on all altcoin transactions.

Moneybit: Which means that most merchants will either stop accepting altcoins, or people will stop purchasing with them. Or both.

K: True. But this might end up being a disadvantage to them in the long run. It'll push altcoins onto the black market.

Moneybit: You mean the real free market.

K: I stand corrected, yes, the free market. Prices will spike and altcoins will become more popular than ever!

Moneybit: The best of times.

K: And the worst of times. Symphy, end transmission. I can't stand to listen to these presstitutes any longer than necessary.

Hologram disappears.

Scene 2

General Small is talking to Sir Hugo Trax via holocall in General Small's office at CIA headquarters.

Trax: Did you find bugs in your office?

Small: Yep! We found a ton of em!

Trax: I can only imagine how those magically appeared. And don't act so boisterous when you're announcing that our communications have been compromised.

Small: Yes, sir.

Trax: Anyway, I assume they've been destroyed.

Small: Yes, sir.

Trax: So now that Bong doesn't have access to our systems anymore, we need to find a way to get him to England.

General Small: You want me to do what?

Trax: Get Bong to England.

Small: You're in London. I'm in the US. Why do you need my help?

Trax (facepalming): Good point. I don't know why I should ever ask you for help on anything. I don't even know why I keep you around.

Small: Because you know that whoever takes my place will be just as incompetent.

Trax: True enough. Ok, back to Bong. Do you have any ideas on how to lure him here?

Small: Well, I always like a good honeytrap.

Trax: I'm sure you do. Bong is too smart for that, though.

Small: How about this? We could spot him on grid surveillance and send a team after him.

Trax: We can't just attack a super spy out in the open like that. We'd get way too much unwanted attention.

Small: We could threaten his loved ones.

Trax: He's a loner, remember?

Small: How about a bribe?

Trax: Your ideas, amazingly enough, are getting worse. Unlike us, he has morals. Bribes are out of the question.

Small: What can we give him that he wants?

Trax: I think I've got it. He doesn't have loved ones, but he does have moral principles that he cares about.

Small: Moral what?

Trax: Yes, nearly a foreign language to guys like us, I know. Anyway, I've got an idea for the perfect bait. See ya, Small.

Small: Wait! You're not gonna tell me?

Trax: If I need something screwed up, I'll call you.

Scene 3

James Bong is sitting at the bar and lounge in the Seehof Hotel in Davos, Switzerland. He is alone with the bartender.

Bong (to bartender): Another scotch and soda, please.

Bong stirs the ice with his finger in the empty rocks glass in front of him as he stares sadly and blankly into space. A striking, young female dressed to impress approaches Bong.

Female: Is this seat taken?

Bong (continues distant stare): The entire bar is taken.

Female (to bartender): I'll have what he's having. (sits next to Bong) You're a very wanted man in London, you know.

Bong (glances at female): I'm a very wanted man in many places.

Bartender delivers drinks. Bong gulps his down.

Female (amused): You've crossed some very influential people in certain circles. They're trying to find a way to get you to London quietly.

Bong (amused): The ever-nebulous "they".

Female: Do you know who I am?

Bong: Mary Poppins.

Female: Diana Gateschild.

Bong turns and looks her up and down.

Bong: They sent you to find me?

Diana (scoffing): Hardly.

Bong: Then what are you doing here?

Diana: I came here to warn you.

Bong: Warn me about what?

Diana: To not go to England. Not on their terms, at least.

Bong: They can murder me anywhere in the world. Why is England so damn special?

Diana: Because they know about your past and want to keep things localized and quiet. They might also think that you can be turned.

Bong: And how do you know all this?

Diana: Because members of the ruling class can be exceedingly paranoid and take certain precautions.

Bong: You mean you spy on each other.

Diana gives knowing smile.

Bong: And why are you helping me?

Diana: Because I want to do what's right.

Bong: How touching.

Diana (stands up): Look, James, my gut tells me that at some point you'll want to confront your past. When that time comes, you can go to England on your own terms and have a chat with the Gateschild brothers. At least if you go on your own terms, you can surprise them and have a chance at survival. But until then, be weary of any temptations they might throw your way. My father can be very clever. Goodbye, James. I'll be watching you.

End Episode 8

Episode 9

Scene 1

At K's place in Acapulco, Mexico.

K (face of befuddlement): Bong.

Bong (amused): K.

K: So let me get this straight. You were just sitting around at some random bar, soaking your troubles in a chilled glass of liquid confidence, and then Diana Gateschild shows up.

Bong: Well, it wasn't like I was at a dive bar. I was at one of the finest resorts in Switzerland.

Moneybit: Bong, I had no idea you were so hoity-toity!

Bong: Just because I'm an anarchist doesn't mean I don't like some finer things now and then.

Moneybit: Then why haven't you asked me out yet?

Bong: K, can you build her a companion and get her off my back? Like a male version of Symphy?

K: Symphy could build another humanoid a lot faster than I could.

Moneybit: Maybe if she weren't so busy being your housekeeper. The place looks great, Symphy! I can finally see the floor!

Symphy: I am much more efficient at cleaning than Master K, so it is only logical that I should be the one to do it.

K: I can't argue there! Ok Bong, back to business. So what do you think Diana Gateschild is up to? Do you think she's telling you the truth, or is she part of her father's scheme?

Bong: Hard to say. Let's say that I believe her, but with a healthy dose of skepticism.

Moneybit: So what's your next move?

Bong: Staying still.

Symphy: That is the most logical move.

Bong (steely): I'm glad that meets your approval.

K: Did you hear about the new tax in England?

Bong: That happens every day. Can you be more specific?

K: The bitcoin purchase tax. Anything bought with bitcoin is subjected to 20 percent tax.

Moneybit: You mean 20 percent extortion.

K: That would be the more precise term.

Symphy: I do not understand taxation. It does not seem logical.

Moneybit: Symphy, congrats. I think you might be the world's first anarchist humanoid robot!

Bong: Yes, K, I heard about the new extortion racket. I don't know how they're going to enforce it, but I have a feeling this is going to cause some major issues in the near future.

K: Speaking of issues….Moneybit, can you unglue yourself from your phone?

Moneybit (coming back to earth face): Huh? What? OH, sorry. I was just checking some posts on Steemit. Have you heard about what's going on down in Uruguay?

K: Where?

Moneybit: Uruguay. Ya know, tiny little country between Brazil and Argentina. Cannabis legalization, dulce de leche, all that?

Bong: Charming place.

Moneybit: Well, it looks like lots of farmers in the northern part of the country are getting forcibly removed from their property!

Bong: Under what pretext?

Moneybit: Not sure, but the most prevalent excuse seems to be some version of eminent domain.

K: You mean imminent theft.

Moneybit: I stand corrected.

Symphy: This seems to conflict with mainstream news reports I'm checking now.

K: Elaborate.

Symphy: It seems that most reports are championing a voluntary "Earth Relocation Project" as a victory for Agenda 21. This does not seem logical to have such conflicting reports.

K: It makes perfect sense if there's an ulterior, and likely sinister, motive. Bong, looks like you can't stay still. Sorry, buddy.

Bong: I vote we send Symphy and I stay here and drink margaritas.

Moneybit (hands on hips): Bong!

Scene 2

General Small's office at CIA headquarters. General Small is meeting with private contract agent Ty Prince.

General Small: I appreciate you rushing up here from South America. I know you were busy down there, but this is quite urgent.

Ty Prince: My crew down there can handle things without me for a while. Are you sure we should be meeting at your office like this? I mean, I'm not officially employed by the CIA, ya know.

General Small: Oh, relax, will ya? We're the only ones here.

Ty Prince: Well, it's just not very clandestine of you.

General Small (sighing): Whatever. Look, let's get down to business. Some very powerful people want Bong brought to England.

Ty Prince: That's a tall order. Remember, I didn't even graduate spy school.

General Small: Yes, yes, I know. I didn't bring you here because you're smart. I brought you here because you're the best brute I've got. At least, that's expendable, that is.

Ty Prince: Thank you, sir.

General Small: But they don't want him brought by force. They want him lured there. Tricked.

Ty Prince: Ya lost me.

General Small: I didn't finish. I think it's a terrible idea and don't see why it's necessary. Which brings me to why you're here. I want you to just find him and kill him.

Ty Prince: Now that I can do. But won't you get in trouble?

General Small: Maybe, but I doubt it. I've got an ace up my sleeve, ya see.

Ty Prince: Won't I get in trouble?

General Small: You might, but that's not my problem. We have a deal?

Ty Prince: What's the price?

General Small (slapping head): Silly me! I forgot to mention the price. What do you think is fair?

Ty Prince: At least a million.

General Small: Do you take checks?

Ty Prince: I'm not that stupid.

General Small: Of course not. Ok, a million cash. But this is between us, a private deal. Nobody else. Got it?

Ty Prince: Got it.

Scene 3

24 Hours Later At Hyde Park, London

Sir Hugo Trax: Small hired you to kill Bong?

Ty Prince: Yes, sir. Small is an idiot, but he thinks I'm an idiot, so I use that to my advantage.

Trax: Yes, Small is obviously an idiot. You're not the brightest bulb on the tree, either. You didn't even pass your final exam for secret agent training.

Ty Prince: I remember!

Trax: Right, well, what now, eh? (looks thoughtfully off into the distance)

Ty Prince: I can kill Small if you'd like, sir.

Trax: No, that won't be necessary. At least, not at the moment. Thanks for telling me this. It's quite useful information. You'd better be getting back to South America, I suppose.

Ty Prince: If that's where I'm needed most.

Scene 4

2 days later…...James Bong is sipping mate at a small restaurant in the town of Artigas, the northernmost town in Uruguay.

Bong (glaring anxiously at smartwatch): Damn you, K. Put down the VR headset game and answer.

K: Hey Bong. Sorry, I was in a heated battle.

Bong: Simulated battle, I suppose. Time to help me in the real battle.

K: What's that noise?

Bong: It's windy as all hell here.

K: It sounds like you're in some sort of wicked sci-fi vortex or something.

Bong (sighing): Anyway, I've been talking to some of the locals. Big surprise news flash, the lamestream media is completely lying. BNN at its worst.

K: So what's really happening?

Bong: My main contact here is a farmer named Marcelo. His family has been here for generations so he knows the ins and outs of everything. He said that the government in Montevideo tried to evict him recently, but he resisted. Recently, however, private mercenaries have been doing the dirty work, and tons of people have been evicted. And I'm talking very large numbers, maybe 10 percent of the state of Artigas.

K: That's epic.

Bong: Indeed. Now get this. The local government goons are telling guys like Marcelo that the reason for their eviction is they are violating some kind of environment code. But he said it's total BS. He suspects the real reason is that part of the Guarani Aquifer, the second largest aquifer in the world, sits under northern Uruguay.

K: Incredible.

Bong: But here's the real kicker. Guess what corporation controls the other parts of the aquifer in Brazil, Argentina, and Paraguay?

K: Aquifers R' Us?

Bong (grimacing): Nice try. No. Angel Water.

K: Angel Water? Wait, aren't they owned by?...

Bong: Machiavelli Bank owns the majority stake, yes. Another path that leads to the Gateschilds.

K: Wow. Have you been taping?

Bong: Yep. I'll send it ASAP. But don't post anything until we fend off the goon squad. I need the element of surprise on my side.

K: You got it. Anything else?

Bong: More 3D printers with a full array of defense programs. Oh, and a raincoat.

K: A raincoat?

Bong: If you ever come to Uruguay, you'll understand.

End Episode 9

Episode 10

Scene 1

Bong is in a field in Uruguay, training Marcelo and other locals on self-defense tactics so that they might repel Angel Water's mercenaries, led by Ty Prince.

Bong: Marcelo, you've never shot a gun?

Marcelo: No, most people here in Uruguay haven't. Most people here are against guns.

Bong: And, by default, against a very efficient method of self-defense.

Marcelo: I didn't say I was against guns.

Some people are lined up, all holding guns, and targets are off in the distance.

Bong: All right, we haven't got much time. I've already shown you the basics. Now take aim, and fire one shot.

All of them take aim, fire, and miss badly. Bong double-facepalms.

2 hours later.....

Bong: Ok, Marcelo. I think that's enough for today. Now I want to gather some intel before it gets dark. Remember that camp you told me about? Where the mercs are, supposedly?

Marcelo (jittery): You mean that fortress.

Bong: Can you take me there?

Marcelo (laughing nervously): I can, but I don't think that's a good idea.

Bong: Why not?

Marcelo: Because I value my life.

Bong: Fine. Just tell me how to get there.

Marcelo looks at Bong's 3D printed Jaguar.

Marcelo: I don't think you should go in that.

Bong: Why not?

Marcelo: In case you haven't noticed, the roads here are in total ruin, and are much worse farther out in the country.

Bong: Then I'll just have to take your jeep.

Marcelo sighs deeply and hands Bong the keys to his classic, Indiana Jones style Jeep.

Bong (sarcastically): I'll be sure and scratch it up real nice for you.

Scene 2

Bong is slowly approaching Ty Prince's mercenary encampment in the middle of the Uruguayan countryside. The wind is starting to pick up and is whipping quite violently.

Bong (watching with binoculars): They've got tents? Not the smartest structure in this windy environment.

Bong feels a sudden sting in the neck and collapses.

1 hour later.....

Ty Prince (looking down on Bong, who is tied to a chair): What luck I have! Look who's fallen into my lap. Hmmm, what to do?

Bong starts to wake up.

Bong (groggy): Prince?

Prince: Bong, who's the smart one now, eh?

A gust of wind causes part of the tent to lift from the ground.

Prince: Damnit! Someone fix the tent again! And do it right this time.

Grunt Worker: But it's too windy, sir!

Prince (pointing finger authoritatively at worker): No excuses!

Bong (sighing): Prince, I should have known.

Prince: What brings you to Uruguay, Bong?

Bong: Your violent theft, unfortunately.

Prince: Oh, look at you, on such a high horse! You used to work the same game, Bong, remember?

Bong: Yes, but I've evolved since then, while you're still mired in darkness. And it's not a game. It's a battle between liberty and slavery. The bottom line is that you're violently stealing people's private property.

Prince: Well Bong, to me it's a game, and one that pays quite well. Now, what to do with you? You know, some very powerful people in London want you brought there. Other people in DC want you dead. Which shall it be, Bong?

Bong: I suppose you'll choose the one that pays the most. You see how easy you are to manipulate? If I pay you the most, I suppose you'd let me go.

Prince (scoffs): As if you can pay more than Machiavelli Bank?

Bong (laughing): Machiavelli Bank, huh?

Prince: Why are you laughing?

Bong: And who in DC wants me dead?

Prince: General Small, of course.

Bong (laughing harder, due to Prince giving him so much info): You are a very, very, stupid criminal.

Scene flashes over to K at his lair in Acapulco.

Symphy: Master K, I've been watching Bong's feed, and it appears he's been captured.

K: Really? The great Bong isn't invincible after all, huh?

Symphy (confused): Human physiology is actually quite frail.

K: It was a figure of speech. Can you link up with his drone fleet?

Symphy: Already on it. Shall I exterminate all life at the camp, other than Bong's?

K (looking at feed on wall screen): Whoa, no, no. Only if it looks like they're about to murder Bong. THC mini-cannons should do the trick.

Scene flashes back to Bong and Prince.

Prince: Bong, I'm going to do you a favor, as much as it pains me to say it. I'm going to spare your life, for now. Now that you're out of the way, I'm sure the locals here will be no match for my squad. (motions to another soldier) You there, take Bong to the gulag!

Soldier (confused): But we don't have a gulag, sir!

Prince: Well, it's about time we did. I'm putting you in charge of the gulag! Now go make one!

Soldier (saluting): Yes, sir!

Prince (surprised, looking up and around): Hey, what's that humming noise? Stop it! You know I hate humming!

Soldier: I thought you hated Karaoke!

Prince: I hate humming and Karaoke!

Scene flashes back to K and Symphy

K: What's taking you so long? They can hear the drones.

Symphy: They're in a tent. I have to cut it open first, before I can fire the THC.

K: OH, right.

Scene flashes back to the encampment. 10 bong-shaped drones are hovering over the giant tent. Four of them are working together to cut open a giant square in the roof of the tent. The giant square of fabric comes loose and is grabbed by robotic arms from 2 of the other drones. The other four drones start firing miniature darts which contain ultra-concentrated THC.

Prince (looking up): We're under attack! Battle stations!

As the soldiers grab their guns and prepare to fire and take cover, they start giggling uncontrollably, and within seconds drop to the ground in a deep sleep.

Bong (looking up at drone, into lens of camera): I'm still tied to this bloody chair. A little help.

K's voice comes over drone's built in speaker....

K: I should leave you tied there for a few minutes, just to teach you some manners.

Bong (rolling eyes): Please untie me.

A drone drops slowly into the tent, hovers near Bong, and a robotic arm cuts the ropes. K yawns and leans back in his cushy office chair.

Bong: I can feel your arrogance from here.

K: That means a lot coming from you.

Symphy (puzzled face): I don't understand why there is animosity between you two.

Bong: It's not your fault Symphy. Nobody understands K.

K: What now, Bong?

Bong: Now I shut off my communications equipment.

Scene 3

The next morning, Ty Prince is having a holo-conference with Sir Hugo Trax.

Trax (furious): You had Bong and let him get away?

Ty Prince: We got ambushed.

Trax (rolling eyes): Oh, likely story. Always with the excuses.

Ty Prince: Easy for you to say, armchair plundering from your cushy little office.

Trax (harsh scowl): Watch it.

Ty Prince: Am I to proceed as planned with the evacuations?

Trax: Absolutely not. We'll need to get Bong out of the area first.

Prince (deep sigh of relief): Whew, that's good.

Trax: Stay in the area and await my orders.

Trax hangs up, grits his teeth, and dials up another number.....

Trax: Bong has turned up in Uruguay. Shall I proceed with Operation Bithouse?

Female Voice: Hugo, darling, is that you? What in the world are you talking about?

Trax (fumbling around): Oh my dear, I'm so sorry. Wrong number.

Trax's Wife: We're having shepherd's pie for dinner, so don't be late!

Trax: Yes dear!

Click.

Trax dials the correct number.

Trax: Bong has caused some problems in Uruguay. Is Operation Bithouse a go?

Gateschild (controlled rage): But of course.

Scene 4

Bong is talking to Marcelo at Marcelo's ranch.

Bong: I'm sure there won't be any problems for you for a while. I've got to be on my way, at least for now. Will you and your friends and neighbors please, at the very least, learn how to shoot straight?

Marcelo: I can't promise we'll ever shoot straight. All I can say is that we'll keep trying. Thanks for your help, Bong. And thanks for not scratching my jeep.

Bong: I guarantee that those who seek to steal your property won't give up, so stay vigilant.

Marcelo: Is there anything I can do for you to show my gratitude? Some mate, or dulce de leche, or some high quality cannabis?

Bong (smiling): No, that won't be necessary. I don't smoke, contrary to popular belief.

Scene 5

One week later at K's hacker lair in Acapulco.....

Miss Moneybit: Wow! That's amazing!

K: You figured out how to use the remote?

Miss Moneybit (punches K in the shoulder): No! That video of Bong's capture in Uruguay is the most popular we've had yet!
Bong: That's very comforting.

K: I'm sure it's because you got rescued, not because you actually got captured. Everyone loves a daring rescue.

Bong (sarcastic): Yeah, real daring, from thousands of miles away with remote controlled drones.

Symphy: Sorry to interrupt, but there is breaking news from the BBC that you will probably find important.

K: Put it on the wall screen.

A huge video pops up on the wall displaying rapid video snippets of people being escorted out of their homes at gunpoint.

BBC Audio: In what the government calls a crackdown on black market sales, those who purchased homes with Bitcoin within the past 10 years are being audited. If they can't pay the new 20 percent Bitcoin commerce tax, they are losing their homes. Many are up in arms over the aggressive government actions, but government officials defend the moves, saying they're necessary to maintain government services now and in the future.

Bong (red faced): Looks like the Gateschilds have made their move. Now I have to make mine.

End Episode 10

Episode 11

In the last episode of James Bong…..Bong and his rag-tag crew received news that in England, the government was stealing people's homes that were purchased tax-free with bitcoin.

Scene 1

James Bong, Miss Moneybit, K, and Symphy are at K's place in Acapulco, discussing their next move.

K: So Bong, you think this is the trap that Diana Gateschild was referring to?

Bong: Yes, obviously. You're not as smart as you look, are you K?

Moneybit: He doesn't even look that smart, to be honest.

K (offended tone): Hey Bong, who's the one with the 150 IQ?

Bong: Mine is 151, actually. And stop rounding up. Yours is 149.

Moneybit: You guys are ridiculous. You both know that IQ isn't a measure of intelligence, anyway. It's not even a very good measure of intellect, actually.

Bong and K narrow their eyes and have a playful stare-down.

Moneybit: Now can we get back on track, please? This is serious business.

K (nonchalant): So they want to kill Bong, what else is new?

Bong (steely sarcasm): I'm glad you take my demise so easily, K.

Moneybit: On the bright side of things, Steem just shot through the roof again, so we've got plenty of resources to work with.

Bong: Good timing. We're going to need them. I suspect they'll be throwing everything they've got at me.

Moneybit: Are you going to actually try and get to the Gateschild brothers?

Bong: I'm going to do more than just that. K, how long will it take you to build another humanoid?

K (fumbling): Oh, um, not long. Maybe a couple months?

Bong: Sorry, genius, that's far too long.

K: But Symphy could build one in just a couple days, I bet.

Symphy: The time I would need to construct another humanoid would be 27 hours.

K: And if I help, I bet we could knock it out in half that time!

Symphy: Actually, Master K, your joining me in the task would actually slow down the process.

Bong (laughing heartily, slapping K on back): Don't worry, K. We'll keep you busy. I'd like a cup of coffee, please.

K (dejected): Very funny.

Bong: But really, K, I'm going to need 2 sets of air and land transport. And let's go with the Aston Martin DB5 this time.

K: Trying to blend in?

Moneybit: How long has it been since your last trip to England?

Bong (gruff): Not long enough.

Moneybit (worried): Bong, please be careful. I've got a bad feeling about this mission.

Bong: Actually, I was planning on being utterly reckless this time. Care to join me?

Moneybit: As tempting as it is to leave Acapulco and go to England in the middle of winter, I think I'll

Bong cuts her off….

Bong: Yeah, yeah, stay here and sip tropical drinks. (stands up to leave) Ok, so I head out in 48 hours.

Moneybit: Where are you going?

Bong: To pick up a winter coat.

K: They don't sell those here in Acapulco, genius.

Bong: Right, I knew that.

Scene 2

At MI6 headquarters, Sir Hugo Trax is having a meeting with General Small.

General Small: Why did I have to come all the way here to help on this mission? I can work remotely, ya know.

Trax: Because if things don't go as planned, I'll need you here as a scapegoat.

Small (rolls eyes): Great. So once we capture him, we're just supposed to hand him over to your boss?

Trax: Our boss, and yes.

Small: I don't even know who our boss is.

Trax: Yes, and we like it that way. It's called compartmentalization.

Small: You and your big words. You know I can't pronounce anything over five syllables.

Trax: Yes, well, enough of your whine festival. Let's review our security details. We've got extra drone fleets with retina recognition guarding the airspace. Have you put extra security at the land crossings?

Small: England is an island. There are no land crossings.

Trax (cringing and huffing): You bloody idiot, we share borders with Scotland and Wales!

Small (confused face): Really? I thought it was just one big bloody island.

Trax: Please don't try and curse with the word bloody. You don't say it right. Anyway, I'll make sure the land borders are secured. As for entry by waterways

Small interrupts

Small: A fleet of man-eating GMO electric eels guarding the coast?

Trax: Bloody hell, no. Where'd you come up with that?

Small: The CIA has had them for decades. They're so cool! They light up like a flashing neon sign when they eat someone.

Trax: Hmmm, perhaps we'll use them when we decide to do away with you, then. As for Bong, no, extra drone boats will suffice. That's all for now. I'll be in the super secret underground command center.

Small: Great, let's go.

Trax: No, no. You're confused again. I'm going to the command center. You go anywhere else.

Small (shaking finger at Trax): Remember the dirty little secret I've got on you. I can shoot the calls anytime I want, so get off your high horse.

Trax (confused): You mean call the shots?

Small: Right, right. Damn jet lag.

Trax: Oh, all right. You can come, but don't touch any buttons.

Small: Got it.

Trax: Or levers.

Small: Ok, ok.

Trax: Or anything that could have consequences anywhere.

Scene 3
2 days later, Bong is flying low in a 3D printed jet, approaching English airspace.

Bong: Putting my life in K's hands yet again. What am I thinking?

K (over Bong's smartwatch): I heard that!

Bong: Stop spying on me. Go back to your video games or whatever it is you do.

K: Ok, but don't come crying to me when ya need help.

Bong sees a fleet of drones approaching.

Bong: Showtime, gotta go.

Click

4 drones surround Bong's jet and start scanning his eyes in order to identify him. After a moment, they allow Bong to continue.

K: See, never fear, K's gadgets are here! Gotta love iris-identity-altering contacts, right?

Bong (grumpy): I swear I turned the smartwatch off.

K: I did some tweaking. You can't shut it off, only I can.

Bong: Brilliant. Just try not to interrupt me, ok, K?

Moneybit: Hi James!

Bong: I can crush this thing with my bare hands, you know? Will that work?

Scene 4

Sir Hugo Trax and General Small are in the super secret MI6 underground command center. It's a giant room with multiple large screens, shiny gadgets and gizmos, but only one other person.
Trax is drinking beer.

Small: Are you sure it's a good idea to be drinking on the job?

Trax (burps): Sure it is. Settles the nerves and makes me forget how much I hate my life.

Small: Well, in that case, mind if I have one?

Trax: No, no, you can't have one. You're dense enough as it is. We don't need you lowering your wits by artificial means.

Small (pointing to the other guy in the room): So, who's that guy?

Trax: He's a lowly computer programming scapegoat.

Guy: I can hear you, ya know.

Small: I thought I was the scapegoat.

Trax; He's the more expendable scapegoat.

Small: Because of the blackmail material I've got on you?

Trax: Exactly.

Guy: I'm just gonna go use the bathroom for a while.

Trax: I'll join you.

Guy (disgusted look on face): Um, I'll go way upstairs and let you go to the closer one.

Guy scampers out of the room with disturbed look on face.

Trax: Ok, so while I'm gone, if a giant red flashing light comes on and the computer announces that Bong has been apprehended, don't do anything. I'll be right back, ok?

Small: Got it. Do absolutely nothing.

Trax leaves the room and a moment later the alarm goes off.

Small (shielding his eyes): Wow, that's way too bright!

He manages to get a glimpse of the screen and figures out how to shut the alarm off. He then chugs a beer, tosses the empty can under the programmer guy's desk, and leans back with his feet up on the desk and starts daydreaming.

Small: Ha! Me, dense.

Trax enters the room.

Trax: Remind me to send the janitor down here when we leave. I miss anything?

Small: Nope.

Scene 5

Philip is dining with another nefarious character at a Gateschild mansion in the English countryside.

Philip (disgusted look at plate, throws down napkin): Too runny, again. Bloody hell. (calls out across vast dining hall) Damnit, Henry! Get over here!

Nefarious Character: Hard to find good help these days.

Bitter Old Servant Henry (approaches table): Yes, sir?

Philip: You've ruined yet another meal, Henry. You know I like my scrambled brains on toast well done. These are runny as all hell.

Bitter Old Servant Henry: I do apologize, sir. Shall I take the plate away?

Philip: Yes, old fool, I can't eat this mush.

Bitter Old Servant Henry: Yes, sir. (turns to walk away and mumbles under his breath) He's got scrambled brains. Why not just eat those?

Philip: What was that, Henry?

Henry: Just a terrible cough I've had recently, sir.

Philip: That's one very unique cough.

Henry walks away.

Nefarious Character: No sign of Bong yet?

Philip: No, but not to worry, he'll turn up. He can't resist helping the poor old tax slaves from losing their little shacks.

Nefarious Character: Are you sure we're not being too aggressive taking homes through violent measures so quickly and out in the open?

Philip: Oh, you worry too much. What are they gonna do? They've got no guns and no guts. They just put their heads down and march off to the slaughterhouse, or the poor house, whichever comes first.

Henry approaches them again.

Henry: Sir, there's someone here to see you.

Philip: Not now, Henry! Can't you see I'm busy?

Henry: Actually, no, I can't see that. It looks like you're just rambling away. Shall I tell them to come back another time, sir?

Philip: Yes, I've got a busy night ahead. Whoever it is, they'll have to wait.

Henry: Very well, sir. I'll tell James Bong to come back at a more convenient time.

Philip (startled): Bong? James Bong is here?

Henry: Yes, sir. But I'll tell him to bugger off.

Philip: No, no! That's all right, send him right in!

Henry leaves.

Philip (smug): Well, that was fairly fast, I'd say! Good old boys at MI6, nothing gets past them!

Nefarious Character: We'll finally meet face to face. It's time to see my son again, after all these years.

Philip: Yes, indeed. Should be a happy occasion. Hopefully I won't have to shoot him.

Scene 6

Meanwhile, back in Acapulco.....

K: Symphy, you've got the broadcast feed ready?

Symphy: Yes, Master K.

K: And the swarm is ready?

Symphy: No, master K.

K (astonished): What? Why not?

Symphy: Just joking. (does robotic laugh)

K: Bad time to joke, Symphy. But hey, I'm glad you're experimenting with humor.

Moneybit: You think this is gonna work?

K (overconfident tone): Sure, no sweat.

Symphy: I estimate a 60 percent chance of failure.

Moneybit: When you say failure, you mean….

Symphy: James Bong dies.

End Episode 11

Episode 12

Scene 1

James Bong is being shown into the enormous dining room of Philip Gateschild by Henry, the old and bitter butler. An old, nefarious-looking character is with Philip.

Henry (at a large entryway, standing with Bong): May I present, Mr. James Bong.

Philip: Yes, a pleasure to meet you Mr. Bong.

Henry: I cooked more scrambled brains for you, sir. Shall I prepare some for Mr. Bong as well?

Philip: No, that won't be necessary Henry. We won't be eating at the moment.

Henry bows, closes the door, and walks away.

Philip: Please, have a seat, Mr. Bong.

Bong sits as he looks at the intricate aesthetics of the room along with the priceless artwork on the walls.

Bong: Please, call me James.

Philip: Very well, James. I'd like you to meet my brother. (motions to nefarious-looking character) This is Jacob Gateschild.

Jacob: A pleasure to finally meet you, James.

Meanwhile, back in Acapulco.....

K (watching a hologram, which is the centerpiece of his techno-lair): This feed is amazing. Crystal clear.

Moneybit: Symphy, this is streaming live on the BBC, right?

Symphy: Affirmative. Everything is going according to plan thus far.

Meanwhile, at BBC headquarters, a shocked and angry program director storms into a production command center....

Director: Can somebody tell me what the hell is going on?

Video Tech (seated at desk): The ratings are going up, sir.

Director: Damnit! That's all fine and good for now, but the BBC president will have my head! I want that feed cut now!

Video Tech: Can't do it, sir.

Director (furious): That's not the right answer. Why the bloody hell not?

Video Tech: The system has been hacked. We're completely locked out.

Meanwhile, at the super secret underground MI6 command center, Sir Hugo Trax, General Small, and a random tech worker are drinking beer.

Trax: We've been down here for so long. I can't believe Bong hasn't shown up in England yet!

General Small: Good thing we've got all this beer. I still feel like I'm forgetting to tell you something.

Random Tech Worker is casually clicking away as he surfs the net….

Worker (eyes pop wide open): Hey guys! Ya gotta see this! BBC is live streaming Bong at the Gateschild mansion!

Trax: That's it, I'm cutting you off.

Worker: No, really! Look!

Trax and Small crowd around the screen.

Small: I just remembered! The alarm went off! That's what I forgot to tell you. It went off when you went to take a leak.

Trax: You mean the alarm that notified us when Bong entered England?

Small: Yeah, my bad. Good thing we've got this random worker here as a scapegoat.

Trax and Small both look at tech worker. Tech worker grimaces.

Meanwhile, at the Gateschild mansion…..

Bong: We need to have a little chat.

Philip: Indeed.

Jacob: I couldn't agree more.

Bong: The main reason I came to see you is that you need to stop stealing people's houses.

Philip and Jacob give each other a look.

Philip: We don't know what you're talking about.

Jacob: We haven't stolen a thing.

Bong: Anyone that bought a house with Bitcoin tax-free is having their house stolen by government agents. With your family holding the controlling interest in Machiavelli Bank, and with your well-known array of government contracts, I suppose it would be in your own self interest to keep the status quo in place, hence your calling in some favors from politicians to get a law passed. A law that attempts to justify stealing the houses of anyone who bought a house in a tax-free manner.

Jacob: A very interesting supposition, James. But there's really no proof, now is there?

Bong: It would be one hell of a coincidence if all of the politicians that voted in favor of this law just happened to receive very large contributions recently, from corporations you control.

Jacob: Oh, James, I really don't see where you get your good little conscience from.

Bong: What's that supposed to mean?

Jacob and Philip share a look.

Philip: Tell him, Jacob.

Jacob: Do you remember your parents, James?

Bong: Of course not.

Jacob: That's because I gave you away when you were a baby.

A knock at the door disturbs them.

Philip (yelling): Not now, Henry!

Henry (yelling through door): Sorry to interrupt, sir! You might want to have a look at the BBC right now!

Philip: I haven't got time to watch one of my propaganda networks right now, Henry! If you disturb us again, it'll be your brains on my platter next time!

Henry: Ok, I tried!

Bong sits with an emotionless expression.

Jacob: You seem to be taking this rather lightly, James. I am your father. You are a Gateschild.

Bong: I'm a Gateschild?

Philip: Jacob, he's obviously in shock. Go on with the rest of it.

Jacob: Now see here, James. All of your exploits over the past few months have been quite unsettling to the family, and the family business.

Bong: Your family business is built on the pain and suffering of others.

Jacob: I'm so sorry you see it that way, James. (picks up briefcase from floor and opens it, revealing stacks of violence-backed pound sterling)
Bong: What's that for?

Jacob: You're part of the family, James. Let's just call it a peace offering. Not only this, but I'd be willing to make you a silent partner in some of our corporations. The only thing you have to do is leave our business dealings alone, unhindered. What do you say, son?

Bong: I say I don't want your immoral, fraudulent, violence-backed paper. I say you make some calls and stop stealing private property.

Philip and Jacob share amused looks.

Philip: Don't you get it, James? We're not taking people's property. Individuals who follow orders, like tax agents and police, are taking that property. They're the ones running around with guns and being aggressive. Not us. Getting to us, James, won't do a damn bit of good for the commoner. They steal from each other.

Bong: That's true, albeit on your command.

Jacob: Are you sure you won't reconsider our offer?

Bong: No deal.

Jacob pulls a pistol out.

Bong: You can't bribe me and you can't scare me. Do you know why?

Philip: Oh, spare us the theatrics.

Bong: Pull the trigger and find out.

Jacob: I hate to do this, son, but you leave me no choice.

Jacob pulls the trigger and shatters Bong's face. Much to the Gateschild's surprise, tiny artificial fragments explode out from Bong's face, thus destroying the humanoid look-alike decoy.

Jacob: What the hell!? It was a ruse! What should we do?

Philip: I'm gonna raise hell with Trax, that's what!

At that moment, a video of the real Bong starts streaming on the BBC.

Bong: Good evening, free humans. I'm James Bong. If you're watching this, that means that you probably just witnessed my humanoid twin confronting the Gateschild brothers. You have also heard them admit to some of their evil deeds. I'm doing what I can to help gain liberty for humans, which at this point in time, is severely lacking. Some of you have been threatened with theft of your homes if you purchased them voluntarily and tax-free with Bitcoin. A tax is nothing more than extortion, and you have the right as free humans to voluntarily exchange goods and services without being extorted by a third party. All of you who have received such threats from immoral individuals, who euphemistically call themselves government agents, will have a package dropped on your doorstep at some time tonight. In this package, you will find a very efficient tool for self-defense called a gun. In order to be free, you must defend yourself and your private property. Liberty is a choice, but so is slavery. Which will you choose?

Scene cuts to Trax and Small, who have been watching the BBC feed……

Trax (facepalming): I'm a dead man.

Small: Gotta die sometime.

Trax's phone starts ringing.

Trax: Hello, Mr. Gateschild. I have good news. We found Bong! He's at BBC headquarters, and we're surrounding the building as we speak! We've got him this time, sir.

Gateschild: How do you know he's at BBC?

Trax: Well, he made kind of an appearance, you might say.

Gateschild: I want more than just the BBC surrounded. I want all possible ways in and out of the country completely sealed for the next 24 hours and every man you've got looking for Bong!

Trax: Yes, sir.

Incoherent yelling and rage can be heard on Trax's phone from Small's perspective. Small takes a deep breath and grimaces. Trax hangs up.

Small: Why'd you tell him you found Bong?

Trax: Well, I had to tell him something, now didn't I? At least it bought me some time.

Scene cuts to the Gateschild mansion

Philip (yelling): Henry! What did you say was so urgent on the BBC?

Henry (yelling back): James Bong was on!

Philip: Damn!

Henry: I tried to tell you!

Philip: Shutup you bitter old goat!

Philip starts to leave.

Jacob: Where are you going?

Philip: Anywhere but here.

Philip and Jacob both leave. Shortly after their departure, the real James Bong swoops in through one of the windows and starts installing hidden surveillance equipment. Meanwhile, thousands of drones can be seen making deliveries to excited and shocked people all over England.

Back in Acapulco, K and Miss Moneybit high five each other.

Symphy: Why the display of elation?
K: Cuz we did it! We pulled it off! The Gateschilds are going down, and liberty is coming up!

Symphy: Must I remind you that James Bong has still not departed Britain safely?

K gives a disapproving look.

Miss Moneybit (to K): Hey, you're the one who programmed her.

Symphy: There is an incoming quantum-encrypted call.

K's eyes bug out.

K: Ok, put it through, I guess.

Female Voice: Is this K?

K: Who's this?

Female Voice: Diana Gateschild.

K (shocked): How did you get this number?

Diana: Short answer, because you're not as smart as you think you are.

Miss Moneybit (sour face): Oooooo, one fried ego, coming right up.

Diana: I need you to get me through to James. They're not allowing exit from the country until Bong is found.

K: So what, you want some prize for turning him in?

Diana (sighing): I can't deal with you right now. Put Moneybit on.

Moneybit: I'm right here!

Diana: How do you deal with him?

Moneybit: I think of it as an art form.

Diana: Anyway, I'm going to help Bong escape, but I need to contact him.

Moneybit: K, send her the number!

K: Can't send to a quantum encrypted phone!

Diana (clicks button to unblock phone): Such a whiny little fellow. (ends call)

Just as Bong is hustling away from the Gateschild mansion, he gets a call…..

Bong: Bad timing, K. I'm a little busy.

Diana: Bong, it's Diana. They're not allowing anyone to exit the country.
Bong: Then I guess I'll have to use some righteous force.

Diana: They'll kill you on the spot.

Bong: And make me a martyr? I don't think so.

Diana: It doesn't have to be that way, James. Let me help you.

Bong (smug): You handy with a machine gun?

Diana: You're such a brute, sometimes. No. As with all government actions, certain people get special privileges. You can fly out on my private jet. They won't give it a thought.

Bong: I'm sure your family will appreciate that.

Diana: I'm trying to do the right thing, Bong. Damn my family to hell. You're still near Philip's house?

Bong: House, castle, creepy monstrosity, whatever you like to call it.

Diana: I'll pick you up within the hour. Leave your phone connected to mine so I can find you.

30 minutes later, a black stretch limo pulls up near Bong.

Diana (speaking out window): Best looking hitchhiker I've ever seen.

Bong gets in.

Bong: So where are we off to? MI6 headquarters to say hi?

Diana: We can if you'd like. I thought you'd prefer my private airstrip.

Bong: Very well, have it your way.

Awkward silence.

Bong: Why didn't you tell me?

Diana: Tell you what?

Bong: That my father is Satan incarnate.

Diana: I wanted to, James, but I didn't feel it was my place to do so.

Bong: Do you know who my mother is?

Diana: No, James, I swear. I don't think anybody does. You see, the reason Jacob gave you up was because your mother was, how can I put this, from a different social class.

Bong: You mean she wasn't a power mad psychopath?

Diana: Precisely. And anyone in Jacob's position would have done the same thing. Give the child up and make sure the mother stays quiet.

Bong: And how does one make sure of that?

Diana: There are different ways. Murder, bribery.

Bong: I suppose asking nicely doesn't make the list.

Diana: You pulled quite the stunt today, James. You're changing the world for the better. I believe we'll have a revolution on our hands.

Bong: I'm not interested in revolution. A revolution brings you around in a circle and you end up at the same spot. What I want is an evolution, where change actually happens.

An hour later and Bong is flying alone on Diana's private jet. As the jet is leaving British airspace, a fleet of immigration control drones approaches the jet, scans for identification, sees that it's Diana Gateschild's private transport, and lets it pass.

Two days later in Acapulco, Bong, Moneybit, K, and Symphy are browsing through an immense number of news stories about the earth shaking events in the UK.

K (reading headlines): Tens of billions pulled out of Machiavelli Bank within 48 hours.

Moneybit (reading headlines): Banking collapse imminent?

Bong (reading headlines): Government postpones Bitcoin housing seizures. Crypto currencies skyrocket, with Steem leading the way.

Symphy holds up hand to prepare for high five.

K: What is it, Symphy?

Symphy: Is this not an appropriate time for a high five?

Moneybit (high fives Symphy): More than appropriate. It's absolutely perfect!

End Episode 12

Episode 13

Scene 1

General Small is in his office at CIA headquarters having a holo-meeting with Sir Hugo Trax.

Small: Look on the bright side, sir.

Trax (incredulous): Bright side? Please, do tell. James Bong just made us look like fools, the Gateschild's bank is collapsing, and now I've got to deal with your smug little face this early in the morning.

Small: Don't be so negative. At least you didn't get fired, and neither did I. Speaking of fired, did that one scapegoat you had strategically placed in the underground command center get fired or killed?

Trax: Nah. I figured, what's the point? It's not like Gateschild is stupid or anything. He'd never believe that one lowly programmer could have been responsible for such an epic security failure.

Small: So how shall we proceed, sir?

Trax: Perhaps we've been going about this the wrong way. There is a key element to Bong's success that I think we've been neglecting.

Small: His superior intellect?

Trax: No.

Small: Physical prowess?

Trax (annoyed): NO.

Small: His morality, courage, and loyalty?

Trax: You're getting warmer, but still no. Bong doesn't publish his own material. If we can silence his publisher, we might be able to swing things back in our direction.

Small: You're talking about Miss Moneybit?

Trax: Exactly.

Small: She disappeared, remember?

Trax: Then we'll just have to make her reappear.

Scene 2

K is playing video games and listening to outrageously loud electronic music.

Symphy (shouting over music): K, Miss Moneybit is at the front door!!

K: Let her in!

Miss Moneybit walks in, covering her ears.

Moneybit (shouting): Turn the music down!!

K: What?!

Symphy turns the music down.

Moneybit: It's 9:30 in the morning! What the hell are you doing?

K: Playing video games and drinking coffee.

Moneybit: And destroying your equipment with bass tones?

Symphy: I have set the sound levels to ensure that no damage is done.

Moneybit looks at holo-screen video game display.

Moneybit: Is that Bong on screen?

K: Yep.

Moneybit: You made a James Bong video game?

K (proud): Yep. I'm doing a test run on it right now. Gotta make sure there aren't any bugs before you market it.

Moneybit (hands on hips): Oh, you're volunteering me to advertise for you, huh?

K: And sell.

Moneybit: Where is Bong, anyway?

K: Don't know. He disappeared.

Symphy: I estimate a 73 percent chance that he is at a casino.

K (sarcastic): Pretty brilliant, Symphy. Moneybit, what's the deal? Why are you looking for Bong?

Moneybit: I'm thinking about taking a trip to DC.

K (surprised): What? You know you can't go back there. The deep state's on the lookout for you in the USSA. You know that.

Moneybit (sighing): Yeah, but I miss my family. And I left a lot of my stuff up there, too.

K: So that's why you want Bong, to go up there with you and protect you.

Moneybit (fidgety): Sorta.

K (brash): I could do it, ya know.

Moneybit starts laughing hysterically at the preposterous idea of a skinny little hacker like K playing body guard.

K: Hey, I've got a white belt in karate.

Moneybit: Isn't that the first belt you get, just for signing up?

Symphy: Affirmative.

Moneybit: Anyway, did Bong say when he'd be back?

K: He didn't even tell me he was leaving. You know how he is. Besides, he just found out he's the son of a Gateschild, which is about like Luke finding out his dad was Darth Vader. Kinda a hard pill to swallow, so what did ya expect?

Moneybit: And Diana Gateschild got murdered, too. That was rough for him. Speaking of the Gateschilds, how is your hack going?

K (bright and cheery): Glad you asked! All the devices Bong planted at the Gateschild mansion are working perfectly. Now we just have to wait for them to fire up a device anywhere in the vicinity, and I'll be able to grab some more dirty little secrets.

Moneybit: We've gotta keep going at them. Did you hear about the bailout?

K: No, what bailout?

Moneybit: The UK government is considering a bailout of Machiavelli Bank so it doesn't fully collapse.

K (huffing): I gotta hand it to the establishment. They're some brazen sons'a bitches.

Scene 3

James Bong is playing blackjack at The Black Spade Casino in Macao. He's been on a hot streak and has grabbed the attention of the security team.

In the security control room…..

Video watchman (speaking to supervisor): Our iris scanners don't say so, but I know that face, sir. I believe that's James Bong.

Supervisor: Really? How do you know?

Video watchman: You didn't see what happened in London last week?

Supervisor: I heard something about it, but didn't watch it.

Video watchman: Should we alert the proper authorities?

Supervisor: Yes, I'll make the call. I'm sure he's a person of interest. Pick him up.

Bong (sips cocktail, talking to dealer): My first time at a blackjack table, and what do ya know?

Dealer (disbelieving): First time high roller, huh?

Bong (sees security personnel in peripheral vision): Perhaps my luck is about over.

Bong tosses a tip to the dealer and starts zig zagging through the casino. He pulls a prepaid phone from his pocket, sends a quick text, ditches the phone, and then makes for the exit. When he leaves, there is a gang of dark suits waiting for him.

Suit #1 (gestures to black limo): Right this way, Mr. Bong.

Bong (sarcastic): No thanks, I've already got plans.

All the suits reach for their sidearms tucked in their jackets.

Bong: On second thought, do you have any vodka in there?

Bong gets in the limo and it speeds off.

Bong: Is this the high roller treatment?

Suit #1: There is someone very important who wants to meet you.

Bong (steely): Another violent psychopath like you, perhaps?

Suit #1: I hope you will show more respect to your host than you have shown me.

Suit #1 whacks Bong in the head and knocks him out.

Scene 4

Washington DC suburbs. Ty Prince is sitting in a posh house waiting for the owner to come home. He's raiding the fridge.

Ty Prince (gawking around large fridge): Man, this guy has got everything! There must be ten different cheeses in here!

Prince hears front door open. He goes to confront the owner.

Male Owner: Who the hell are you?

Prince: I'm Ty Prince.

Male Owner: What the hell are you doing in my house?

Prince (casually): Holding you for ransom.

Owner dashes for front door.

Prince: I'm pointing a pistol at your head.

Owner stops in his tracks. Prince is searching madly for his pistol in the living area. Owner turns around and sees Prince's desperation. Prince finally locates the pistol on the floor and points it for real this time.

Prince: You're Marty Moneybit, right?

Owner: Nope, wrong house.

Prince: I don't believe you. Show me your ID.

Owner: Ok, ok, yes, I'm Marty Moneybit. What the hell is this all about?

Prince: You'll find out soon enough. Take a seat. It's gonna be a long night.

Marty: You're Ty Prince?

Prince: The one and only.

Marty: Yeah, I heard about you. You're not the smartest criminal, huh?

Prince: Shut your trap. I need you to make a call.

Marty: Which do you want, me to shutup or make a call? I can't do both. Well, I guess I could do both, but if I don't say anything, then the other person will definitely hang up.

Prince sighs.

Scene 5

K's place in Acapulco. K and Moneybit are playing Bong's video game and drinking tequila.

Moneybit: It really looks just like him. You're really good at what you do, K.

K: Thanks. Something tells me you've had too much tequila.

Moneybit: Why's that?

K: Because you're smiling and complimenting me.

Symphy walks in.

Symphy: K, there is a message from an unidentified phone. The message simply says "420".

K: Whoa! That's Bong! Can you trace the call?

Symphy: I am working on it.

K: Let me know ASAP.

Moneybit's phone starts ringing. It's a Blondie "Call Me" ringtone.

K: I see I'm not the only 80s music lover here.

Moneybit (to phone): Hi, dad?

Marty: Hey, little lemon.

Prince speaks in background: You call her little lemon? Worst nickname ever!

Miss Moneybit (surprised): Dad, who's that?

Marty: Ty Prince.

Prince (yelling): I told you not to say that!

Miss Moneybit: What?! What's going on?

Marty (nonchalant): He's pointing a gun at my head, eating all my cheese, and threatening to kill me if you don't come to DC. Don't come, though. He's not that smart, so I think I can take him.

Prince: Not if I shoot you in the leg first.

Miss Moneybit (crying): Oh my God, dad! I'm coming right away! Just, just.....

Marty: No! I'm telling you, they're not gonna get to my little girl. I'll be fine. You stay safe!

Prince (yelling): Are you coming or not?!

Miss Moneybit hangs up and starts walking out.

K: Where are you going?

Moneybit: To DC, of course.

K: Hold on. Let's think of a plan first.

Moneybit: And let my dad suffer?

K: Just at least let me track down Bong first.

End Episode 13

Episode 14

Scene 1

Bong has just been thrown into a secret Chinese cage by some underworld mafia figures. There is one other prisoner in the cage.

Bong (groggy): I wasn't expecting company.

Prisoner (grumpy): You won't be getting any, don't worry.

Bong: How long have you been in here?

Prisoner: I've lost track of time.

Bong: Why are you here?

Prisoner: You first.

Bong: I won a couple hundred thousand at a blackjack table, but I have a curious feeling that there's more to it than that.

Prisoner: Who are you?

Bong: Bong, James Bong.

Prisoner (sarcastic): Oh yeah? And I'm Peter Pipe.

Bong: No, that's really my name. You haven't heard of me?

Prisoner: So modest of you. Anyway, you can call me Punch.

Bong: Like fruit punch?

Punch (offended): No, not like fruit punch! Like punch you in the face punch.

Bong: You still haven't told me why you're here.

Punch: Why should I trust you?

Bong: If you haven't noticed, we're both locked up. Circumstances dictate that we cooperate and maybe find a way out of here.

Punch: They're trying to milk me for info.

Bong: What kind of info?

Punch: I know a guy they'll do anything to get to. An inventor. I won't give up his location, though. Hopefully he can get that tech out before they get to him.

Bong: Who exactly are "they"?

Punch: Anyone and everyone in the energy business.

Bong: I was nabbed by Triads, I believe. They have heavy interests in Chinese casinos. What does the Chinese mafia have to do with the energy business?

Punch (shaking head): Man, were you born yesterday? Triads do business with the Chinese government and global corporations everywhere. They do things that the military agencies can't.

Bong: So what's this invention they're so desperate for?

Punch: A new energy source. Free energy. Can you imagine? So why the hell did they grab you?

Their conversation is interrupted by a couple of guards.

Guard: Bong! You're coming with us.

Bong: Dinner time already? What's on the menu?

Guard: Smoked Bong, funny guy.

Scene 2

Meanwhile, at K's place in Acapulco

Symphy: Bong's communication came from Macao.

K: All the casinos on this side of the world and he's gotta go to China for his gambling fix.

Moneybit: I can't wait around for Bong's help. I've gotta get to DC to help my dad.

K (emphatic): You can't go to DC. You know it's a trap! They're just trying to get to you!

Moneybit: You got a better plan?

K: Well, no, not exactly.

Moneybit: Then I'm outta here.

Moneybit leaves and slams the front door.

Scene 3

Back in Macao....

Bong is escorted into a huge vaulted parlor, where a young, sharp dressed Chinese man is seated on a red throne.

Sharp Dressed Man: Welcome Mr. Bong. I'm impressed.

Bong: Yeah, I work out.

Sharp Dressed Man: And such humor. Pretty good for a dead man walking.
Bong: I don't follow.

Sharp Dressed Man: Or shall I say a ghost? Have a seat, Mr. Bong.

Bong sits in a rickety wooden chair next to him.

Sharp Dressed Man (motioning to the only two guards in the room): Leave us.

Bong: You're either very bold, or very stupid.

The guards leave. Sharp dressed man punches some buttons and a huge hologram of a Chinese
State news feed pops up.

Sharp Dressed Man: Once you see the offer I'm going to make you, I'm sure that bold will be your
final assessment. Allow me to explain. You see the headline?

Bong: A gang of Chinese psychopaths calling themselves government claim that James Bong is
dead.

Sharp Dressed Man: Why are you so unpleasant, Mr. Bong?

Bong: I have a severe allergy to being thrown in cages.

Sharp Dressed Man: Regardless of your negative qualities, I've been quite impressed with your
work.

Bong: Forgive me if I don't find that flattering, coming from you.

Sharp Dressed Man: Do you even know who I am?

Bong: I know you're a member of the Triads.

Sharp Dressed Man (offended): King of the Triads, actually. You can call me King T.

Bong: You must not follow my work too closely if you think I'll call anyone king.

King T: I've had people executed for less. Show some respect. Anyway, down to business. That
was quite a stir you caused in London. And such a blow to your family, the Gateschilds.

Bong: They're not my family.

King T: Regardless, their bank, Machiavelli Bank has lost billions because of what you did. And I'm sure you know their deep involvement in the energy sector. So now here's the deal. That man you met in your prison cell?

Bong (steely sarcasm): Yes, charming character.

King T: He knows a scientist who has created a marvelous new substance that can produce free energy in near limitless supply.

Bong: And now you want him murdered in order to protect the status quo. This has gone on for centuries.
King T: I would never do such a thing. What I want is to control it.

Bong: And with it, the Gateschilds suffer another crucial blow to their empire.

King T (smug grin): Which would also serve your interests as well.

Bong (scoffing): How? Trading a British gangster clan for a Chinese gangster clan? I hardly see how free humanity gains any ground.

King T: Well, either way, Mr. Bong, you have no choice in the matter. Either you agree to help track down the scientist, or you rot away in prison while the world believes you to be dead. What do you say?

Bong: I say you call your guards back and look for plan B.

King T calls the guards back.

Bong: And by the way

Bong jumps up, grabs King T's head and slams it into the stone table he's seated at.

Bong: You're very stupid, not bold.

Bong grabs a gun from King T's side and rushes over to the entrance. The guards come in. Bong knocks one over the head and shoots the other in the knee. He then looks for the keys to the cell and can't find any. He runs back to the cell.

Punch: They must really trust you, to let you come back by yourself.

Bong: Glad to see you developed a sense of humor while I was away.

Bong sees that the cell is locked with an electronic keypad.

Punch: How good are you at hacking?

Bong: Unspeakably horrible.

Bong runs out.

Punch: I'll just stay here, then.

Bong goes back into King T's parlor. He finds a smartphone on one of the guards and dials K.

Back in Acapulco….

Symphy: You have a message from a phone in Macao.

K: What's the message?

Symphy: 420.

K: Call that phone!

Bong (while running back to the cell): K.

K: Bong, you sound pretty good for a dead guy.

Bong: I need you to pick a lock for me. I'll explain later. What info do you need about it?

K: Just send me a pic and I'll have it done in 5 minutes.

Bong: Make that 2 minutes.

Bong takes a picture and sends it. A couple minutes later, the green light comes on and the cell door pops open.

Bong: Let's go. You're gonna take me to your scientist friend, ok?

Punch: Let's just try to get out of Macao first.

Bong: Deal.

Scene 4

At Moneybit's father's house in DC.

Marty Moneybit (to Ty Prince): She's not gonna come.

Ty Prince: She'll come.

Marty Moneybit: Even if she does, it's gonna take forever. No way you can stay awake that long.

Ty Prince gets uncertain look on face.

Marty: Didn't think of that in your master plan, did ya?

Ty Prince: Shutup! I'm thinking!

Ty Prince's phone rings.

Ty Prince: Hey Sir Trax, whatsup?

Sir Hugo Trax: Don't say my name over the phone! Can your hostage hear you?

Marty: Loud and clear!

Trax (gruff): And you've got me on speaker!? Damnit, Prince! Idiot. Anyway, we're calling off the mission.

Ty Prince (shocked, disappointed): What?! Why the hell are ya doing that?!

Trax: The Chinese are reporting that Bong is dead. Killed himself at a casino. Witnesses and everything. So we're celebrating!

Ty Prince: Has MI6 or the CIA confirmed this?

Trax: Damnit, Prince! Don't mention your employers' names on the phone!

Marty: It's ok! I already knew!

Trax: Anyway, don't be foolish, of course it's confirmed.

Ty Prince: Well, can I at least kill this guy anyway?

Trax: Absolutely not! There's no reason to kill him now.

Ty Prince: He's one hell of a smartass. Isn't that good enough?

Trax: Prince, you have your orders.

Click.

Ty Prince (to Marty): Well, I suppose I'll be on my way. Nice meeting you and all.

Marty gives sarcastic grin. Ty Prince leaves. Marty calls his daughter, Miss Moneybit.

Miss Moneybit: Dad?

Marty: Hey, it's ok. That government thug just left.

Miss Moneybit (shocked): He did? That's great! Why?

Marty: Something about Bong being dead.

Miss Moneybit (confused): What?! I'm on a plane and it's hard to hear you. You said Bong's dead?!

Marty: That's what the guy from MI6 told Ty whatzhisname a minute ago. Then he gave him orders to leave me alone.

Miss Moneybit (crying): Well, oh my god. I'm so happy you're ok, dad, but…

Marty: I know, I understand. Go back to your friends. I'm sure they'll want to see you and talk about Bong. I'm fine.

Miss Moneybit: Thanks, dad.

Marty: Take care, kid.

Click.

Moneybit looks at her phone. It's a text from K, alerting her to the true situation that Bong is in. Moneybit asks the pilot to return to Acapulco.

End Episode 14

Episode 15

Scene 1

Bong and Punch have just escaped the Triad underground prison and are on the move in Macao.

Bong: So where's your inventor friend?

Punch: Central Africa.

Bong: Central Africa? Why Africa?

Punch: They have less electronic surveillance. It's easier to be a ghost. More importantly, Central Africa has resources he needs to make the substance. Resources that don't exist in other parts of the world.

Bong: I don't suppose you have any gadgets handy? Or cash?

Punch (sarcastic): Oh, sure, they let me keep all my personal stuff during my month in prison.

Bong: Any locals you trust?

Punch: Not a soul.

Bong; Why the hell are you in Macao then?

Punch: To stay anonymous, you don't want people around who know you, genius.

Bong: I know a little twerp hacker with an attitude you'd get along with great. Anyway, let's get to a 3D print shop. I've got an idea.

10 minutes later at a 3D print shop, they're talking to an irritable, chain-smoking, shop owner guy.

Bong: I'm telling you, just one text message on your phone, and I'll pay you double for all the printing I need to do here. I just need some funds.

Irritable Shop Owner Guy: Triple!

Bong; Glad to see there are such helpful people left in the world.

Irritable Shop Owner: Take it or leave! This business, not charity!

Bong: Fine, triple.

Shop owner gives phone to Bong. Bong texts K to send funds to the shop owner's crypto account and schematics for everything he needs to print. Once the funds arrive, he prints a new phone, the rest of the supplies he needs, and gets more crypto sent from K to his new phone. He then arranges for a SteemAir Transport to Central Africa.

As Bong and Punch near the airport…..

Punch: So how exactly do you plan to get past security? You realize that if we're wanted by the Triads, then we're wanted by the Chinese Government.

Bong: Yes, I'm well aware, one mafia split into two halves. And I prefer to call government a 'violent gang with fancy titles', by the way.

Punch: You still didn't answer my question.

Bong (reaches into backpack, pulls out two contact lenses): These are iris changing contacts to hide your identity.

Punch: And facial scanners? What about those?

Bong (pulls a pack of tiny adhesive dots from backpack): These are nano-modifiers. You put one on your forehead and it changes the readings on their face scanners.

Punch: And if anyone recognizes us from memory?

Bong: Oh, don't be so paranoid. This is why I like working alone.

Punch: There are things I'd much rather be doing, trust me.

Bong: Anyway….. (reaches into backpack) that's why I've got two fedoras.

Punch: You've got to be kidding.

Bong: Would I really have brought fedoras just to play a prank?

Bong and Punch get through security unnoticed and board their plane without incident. Bong gets into the pilot's seat of the private, hemp-powered, SteemAir jet and they take off. Once they get up to cruising altitude, Bong puts it on autopilot and dials up K.

Bong: K.

K: Bong! You sound good for a dead guy!

Bong: Yeah, gambling and martinis keep me in good order.

K: Someone wants to say hi.

Miss Moneybit (sarcastic): Bong! I really could have used your help a couple days ago. Thanks for being there, old buddy!

Bong: Good to hear you're relieved I'm not dead.

Miss Moneybit: Where ya headed?

Bong: Central Africa.

Miss Moneybit: You have a camera?

Bong: Just the one on the phone. Do I have to record all of my missions?

Miss Moneybit: It is how we finance things, ya know.

Bong: Well, it's gonna be one hell of a story, regardless. I met a guy in a Triad prison who's taking me to meet some inventor-in-hiding, who supposedly has some miracle free energy source.

Miss Moneybit: Triad Prison again?

Bong: Very funny. Long story. I'll update you when we get to Africa.

K: You mean you'll call when you're desperate for help again.

Click

Bong: So tell me more about this energy source.

Punch: I only know the basics. The rest is over my head. It involves some combining organic materials with synthetic materials.

Bong: That's nothing new.

Punch: In a zero g atmosphere.

Bong: I stand corrected. Zero g? How did your friend…

Punch: He used to work for the Chinese Space Agency.

Bong: He worked at an extortion funded space agency. Ok.

Punch: He was doing experiments in zero g, that was his job. Then he discovered the new material quite by accident.

Bong: And why did he flee?

Punch: Luckily, he's not naive. He knows how much power the people that control the energy sector have. He also knows it could be a threat to a huge government's power.

Bong: Like the Chinese criminal enterprise.

Punch: Why do you keep referring to government like that?

Bong: Because it's the truth. And how powerful is this material?

Punch: He estimates it can power the entire planet for one year on one kilo.

Bong: That's definitely a threat to the powers that shouldn't be. So how do you know where to find him?

Punch: We had previously set a rendezvous point. He wanted to work in secret on how to deploy the technology, without being destroyed or compromised.

Bong: Smart man. Didn't want to get Tesla'd, huh?

Punch: Something like that.

Bong: That reminds me, reach behind you and grab that duffel bag. There are gun parts in there and instructions for assembly. I printed them at the shop.

Punch: I don't like guns.

Bong: I guarantee you will when you need to defend yourself.

Punch: How did you get them through security, anyway?

Bong: Because, in case you haven't noticed, security people at airports aren't the sharpest knives in the kitchen.

Scene 2

Bong and Punch are making their descent into the Congo, near a small village called Kungu. After a bumpy landing in a somewhat clear area.....

Punch (sarcastic); Real smooth.

Bong: And where did you learn to fly?

Punch looks at ground.

Bong: That's right, ya didn't. So you're welcome. Anyway, where's this rendezvous point.

Punch: In the village a few miles west of here.

Bong: Kind of a vague "point" isn't it, an entire village?

Punch: It's not like it's huge. It's only a couple thousand people.

Bong and Punch walk to the village. They get some curious looks from the locals.

Bong: You have a picture we can use to ask around?

Punch: Again, it escapes your memory that we just got out of a cage.

Bong: You said he worked for the Chinese Mafia's Space Agency, right?

Punch: Yeah.

Bong: What's his name? I'll try and get a pic online.

Punch: Sun Zen. It would've been scrubbed by now, though.

Bong; I know someone who might be able to find it.

Bong dials up K.

Bong: K!

K: Bong!

Bong: I need you to find a pic for me online.

K: Bong, girls find you attractive. I don't see why you need to

Bong cuts him off.

Bong: Not now, K, this is important! I'm searching for the inventor I mentioned to you before. His name is Sun Zen and he used to work for the Chinese Space Agency.

K: Is that Sun with a "u" or an "o"?

Bong (sighs): Just text it to me when you have it.

Bong spots a whole-in-the-wall bar.

Bong: That'll be a good place to meet locals.

Punch: A bar during the middle of the day?

Bong and Punch walk into the tiny little shack. Two local men and the bartender gape at the newcomers.

Bong: Martini, shaken, not stirred.

Punch: Look at your surroundings, Bong. This doesn't look like a martini-sippin town, now does it?

Bartender: Hey, what do ya mean by that?

Punch: Do you know how to make a martini?

Bartender: Well, I'm a bartender, so what do ya think?

Punch: Sorry, it's just that

Bartender (offended): Yeah, yeah, I know, small town, unsophisticated stereotype. I get it.

Punch: I'll pass on the drink, then.

Bong looks at his phone and shows the picture to Punch. Punch nods to confirm Sun's identity. Bartender sets martini in front of Bong. Bong shows picture to bartender.

Bong: Have you seen this guy around here?

Bartender (smiles): Everybody knows that guy.

Punch: Really? Why is that?

Bartender: It's a small town, man. What do ya think? Everybody knows everybody.

Punch: Isn't that a stereotype?

Bong (huffy): We haven't got time for this. (chugs martini) Can someone take us to him?

Bartender looks at his two local customers.

Bartender: I'm not sure those two are in shape to go up the hill to his house right now, but they maybe could.

Bong: Can one of you take us there?

Local Guy 1: No way. I'm just getting started drinkin.

Bartender: You've been here since we opened.

Local Guy 1: It's not even sunset yet!

Bong: I'll buy you a drink if you do.

Local Guy 1: Make it two.

Bong (annoyed): Fine. Let's go.

Bong, Punch, and the local guy leave. After walking for about 20 minutes they arrive at a small cottage.

Local Guy: There ya go. That's his shack. I'll wait here.

Bong and Punch go to the shack and knock. No answer. Punch yells his name a couple of times. No answer.

Bong: Let's just go in.

Bong turns the doorknob and notices it's not locked.

Bong: That's strange. Why is it open?

The door opens and they immediately find out. Sun Zen's bullet-riddled body is lying on the floor. Bong rushes over and checks his pulse, only to find that he's dead.

Bong: Blood is still fresh. This happened just a short time ago.

Punch (sobbing): We're too late.

Bong: Yeah, we're too late.

After leaving Punch at the Kinshasa airport, he goes back to Acapulco. After telling K, Miss Moneybit, and Symphy about the outcome of his mission…..

Miss Moneybit: Don't beat yourself up over it. You failed. You're human, right?

Bong: Last time I checked.
Miss Moneybit: It happens. I mean, look at K, he's had tons of epic failures.

K: You have a very loose definition of epic.

Bong: Do you realize what kind of opportunity it was? Near limitless energy, practically free.

Symphy: I am sorry to interrupt, but there is news that you might find pertinent to the situation.

K: What's that?

Symphy: I found a blogger on Steemit. The account is less than two weeks old. The name is SunZenergy. The only posts it contains are instructions on how to create a free energy material in a zero g atmosphere.

Bong: What do you mean "found"? Why wouldn't something like that show up in a standard internet search?

K: Because somebody's trying to hide it.

Symphy: K is correct. Great effort is being made to hide this information. Only due to my advanced Artificial Intelligence abilities was I able to find it.

K (talking to Moneybit): Looks like you've got some publishing to do.

End Episode 15

Episode 16

Scene 1

Bong, K, Miss Moneybit, and Symphy are having breakfast at K's place in Acapulco. K is making omelettes and Symphy has just served coffee.

Bong (after taking sip of coffee): Symphy, I wanted coffee, not rocket fuel.

Symphy (confused face): This coffee can certainly not perform the task of propelling a rocket.

K: He was exaggerating, Symphy. And the coffee is great. Bong's just weak.

Symphy: I could process data of human relationships for millions of years and never understand them.

Miss Moneybit (sighs): You're not alone, Symphy. You're not alone.

K dishes up some omelettes and sets them in front of Bong and Moneybit. Moneybit takes a bite.

Moneybit (painful face): Oh, K! What the hell?! What's in this?

K (proud): A variety of the finest hot peppers known to man.

Moneybit: Ah, I can't eat this. It'll put me in the hospital.

K: You're just as weak as Bong.

Bong: I don't know why I spend any of my free time with you guys.

Moneybit: Bong, I think you need a vacation.

Bong: I just had a vacation, remember?

Moneybit: You got kidnapped and thrown in a cage during your so-called vacation, so I don't think that counts.

Bong: Are you trying to get rid of me?

Moneybit: Nope. I'm going with you.

Bong (shudders, chuckles): K, what did you put in this coffee? Moneybit seems to be hallucinating.

Moneybit: Come on, it'll be fun. I'll even pay half the expenses.

Bong: Gee, how generous. (pauses and contemplates) Oh, I suppose I could go for a few days and just do some easy, fun disruptions of the state.

Moneybit: Sounds like work to me.

Bong; It's not work if it's fun. Not in my book, anyway.

Moneybit: Great, it's settled then! We'll take off this afternoon!

Bong: We?

Moneybit: Please?

Bong (reluctant): Oh, all right.

Scene 2

The next morning, Bong and Miss Moneybit are cruising I-10 in Southeastern New Mexico, between Las Cruces and El Paso, Texas. They're riding in a 3D-printed model of a black Aston Martin DB10.

Miss Moneybit: Bong, no offense, but this isn't the vacation spot I had in mind. Why did you choose this place?

Bong: Simple. It's one of the biggest speed traps in the world. Tons of mind-controlled road pirates. Plus, there isn't too much traffic, so it's safer to do what we're doing. And you should be excited!

Miss Moneybit: Why would I be excited to be near a bunch of cops?

Bong: Because we're going to "buzz" them, and free their would-be victims.

Miss Moneybit: Great. I'll get my camera ready!

They soon come upon some flashing red and blue lights, and spot an immoral order-follower ahead. The cop has someone pulled over.

Bong: Sit tight. Statist Road Pirate crime in progress and is about to be thwarted with relish.

Bong accelerates aggressively and as they approach the road pirate and the victim. The uniformed order-follower is approaching the driver's side of the victim's car. Bong carefully veers close enough to the cop to scare him, but not harm him. The Aston Martin roars by at over 100mph.

Road Pirate (shaking fist): Hey, what the hell!? (turns and faces his victim, grumbles and stumbles around, uncertain what to do)

Road Pirate (to would-be victim); Ah, to hell with you. You got lucky this time!

Road Pirate runs back to his car and takes off after Bong and Moneybit. At this point, Bong has it up to top speed, near 200mph. He takes an exit into Las Cruces and makes plenty of turns so they can't be found.

Moneybit: Whew! What a rush!

Bong: Fighting against tyranny can be fun, right?

Moneybit: Wow! My heart feels like, well, if I would drink 5 cups of K's coffee. I wanna try!

Bong (grimaces): Um, not a good idea.

Moneybit: Come on! And you can film it!
Bong (sarcastic): Oh, really, can I?

Moneybit: What could go wrong?

Bong: The imagination runs wild. (pauses) All right. But first, we need a disguise.

Moneybit: I left my masks at home.

Bong: The car. Not us. (does facepalm)

Moneybit: You said "we" not "it".

Bong: This is why I work alone.

Bong hits a button on the dashboard. The car's nano-paint starts to change color, and within seconds, the entire car is red.

Moneybit: Not just your typical, run-of-the-mill Aston Martin, huh?

Bong hits another button.

Bong: New plates from Kansas. That ought to be enough.

Bong and Moneybit change seats. They head back onto I-10 and seek out another road pirate crime in progress. Within minutes, they spot another immoral order-follower with a badge trying to extort a free human.

Bong: Here we go. You see them?

Moneybit: Yep!

Bong (frowning at speedometer): One thing about cars like this, Moneybit, is that they like to go fast.

Moneybit: What?

Bong: Would you mind hitting the gas? We'll be able to have a short chat with him if we crawl by at this pace.

Moneybit (defiant): Be careful what you wish for! (she floors it)

Bong's head snaps back. He pulls out a smartphone and starts filming.

Bong: Please don't hit them.

The car gets up to 110mph and with superb balance and skill, Moneybit maneuvers the Aston Martin to within about 3 feet of the cop, who cowers and leans against his would-be victim's car.

Bong: Wow!

Moneybit: Was that the same road pirate?

Bong: I think so. Keep hitting the gas! We gotta lose him.

Moneybit gets the car up to top speed and after a couple minutes exits into Las Cruces. She pulls into the back of a supermarket parking lot.

Moneybit: Ok, Bong, change the car. Hurry!

Bong changes the car to midnight blue and the plates to New Mexico.

Bong: Now we're local.

Moneybit pulls back onto the street. Bong reviews the video.

Bong: Wow, you look much better on camera.

Moneybit: Thanks, I think.

Bong: Congratulations, you just saved someone from being extorted.

They soon come across a public park and find a group of teenagers being harassed by another order-follower in blue. Bong and Moneybit approach the group.

Bong (to cop): Excuse me. What's going on?

Cop (pompous): This doesn't concern you.

Bong: Quite to the contrary, if natural rights are being violated, it's most definitely my business.

Cop: These kids are smoking something they shouldn't be. Now get lost.

Bong: So they weren't doing anything wrong, but you are.

Cop (looking Bong up and down, skeptically): Hey, wait a minute. I know you from somewhere. (pauses) Yeah, you're that guy from D-tube. You're James Bong! (looks at Moneybit) And you must be his girlfriend publisher, right?

Moneybit blushes.

Bong: Not girlfriend. Anyway, how about leaving these people in peace?

Cop: Look, I'm just doing my job, man. I know there's nothing wrong with what they're doing, but if I don't make arrests, I'll lose my job. I've got a family to feed, ya know.

Bong: You don't need to have a job that involves violence to support your family.

Cop: Yeah, but what can I do?

Bong: Anything that doesn't involve violence. The possibilities are limitless.

Cop (turns to teenagers): You're all free to go.

Bong: Wise choice. I think we'll be going as well.
Cop: Sure, Bong. I'll think about what you said.

Bong and Moneybit get back in the Aston Martin and zoom off.

Bong: You film that?

Moneybit: Yep. You do realize that once this trip is posted online, then the whole world will know you're not dead.

Bong (sarcastic): Really? That hadn't occurred to me. What do you suppose K is doing right now?

Moneybit: Probably listening to 90s rap music and playing holo-Pac-man in his boxers.

Bong: What a horribly vivid picture.

K: I heard that!

Moneybit (startled): K, what the hell?!

Bong: How long have you been listening to us?

K: Long enough.

Moneybit: Creep.

Bong: I specifically didn't bring a smart watch with me, just to avoid situations like this.

K: I know. That's why I hacked the car.

Bong: How quaint.

K: I hate to break up the party, but I think you should both get back down here. There are some big things happening and we need to game plan ASAP.

Bong: What big things?

K: We should talk about it in person, in private.

Bong: You're always so painfully esoteric. All right, we'll fly down tomorrow.

K: Sorry to wreck another vacation of yours.

Bong: No you're not.
Moneybit: Goodbye, K!

K (grumpy): Ok, ok, I'll hang up.

Clicking noise over the speaker.

Moneybit: You think he actually disconnected?

Bong: Not a chance.

Moneybit: Can I fly the plane?

Bong (huffs loudly): Sure, why not? I'll just sip cocktails.

K: I can fly it remotely, ya know!

End Episode 16

Episode 17

Scene 1

Bong and Miss Moneybit walk into K's place in Acapulco.

Bong: Ok, K, what's so urgent that it couldn't wait until my vacation was over?

K: It was the best of times, it was the worst of times.

Bong (narrows eyes): K, must you be so damned esoteric?

Moneybit: He's just trying to be annoying.

Bong: He's being both.

K: Check this out. Let's start with the best of times. There are millions of people in the US and UK refusing to pay income taxes.

Bong: How do you know?

K: Cuz thousands are being quite vocal about it online. Not only that, but the oligarch-owned media is being quiet on the whole subject. Normally, this time of year they're bragging about record tax collections. All they're spouting now is absurd propaganda about "duty to pay taxes".

Moneybit (huffs): Duty to be violently extorted, I don't think so.

Bong: So they're getting desperate.

K: But, like I said, it's also the worst of times. Observe. (clicks on holographic projection) These are the top 50 cryptocurrencies as of this morning. Notice the extreme fluctuations in value for most of them.

Bong: Hundreds, or even thousands of percentage points.

K: Yeah, not exactly models of stability that people can trust. Except for 3 currencies, you'll notice. 3 of them are quite stable and gaining in popularity. Symphy and I did some deep searching and found out that, through various shell companies, the top 3 cryptocurrencies are controlled by Machiavelli Bank, The Carpyle Group, and Saturn Industries.

Moneybit: 3 of the largest corporations on the planet.

Bong: So what are you getting at, K?

K: They're being manipulated to scare people away from real, free market options, and towards options controlled by the entrenched oligarch-controlled institutions.

Bong: But how?

K: Quantum computers.

Moneybit: Quantum computers?

Bong: Can you prove this?
K: Not only can I prove it, but I've got a mission in mind that involves you to stop this madness.

Bong (sarcastic): Another bulletproof plan from K.

K: Symphy finally tracked down where the computer is located, we think. And it wasn't easy to track down a quantum computer, lemme tell ya. If it weren't for Symphy's advanced A.I. system it would've been hopeless.

Bong: What do you mean, you think you tracked it down?

K (cringing): Ya caught that, huh? Ok, so Symphy gives it a 63 percent chance that the quantum computer is located at an underground base in Alaska, under the old Fort Wainwright.

Bong: You expect me to go to Alaska and hunt for a supercomputer based on a 63 percent chance?

Moneybit (mocking): Why not? I would....

Bong: Old Fort Wainwright, huh?

K: Yeah. You know it from the Russian war, right?

Bong (sad): I know more about it than I care to admit. (pauses) Ok, so once I'm there, then what?

K: Symphy's developed some nanobots that should be able to disrupt its operations without destroying it. Once trading normalizes for a few days and people can see more stability, it'll boost confidence. Not only that, but I'll have Moneybit put together a report of how the values are being manipulated. Then we'll show what happens after the banksters are forced to stop their manipulation.

Bong: So I suppose I'm to record all this.

Moneybit: Of course!

Bong: Why Alaska, of all places?

K: Cuz it's cold, and I imagine quantum computers get quite hot.

Bong: All right, K. Get the gear ready. I'll leave tonight.

Scene 2

Jacob Gateschild is dining and having a meeting with Winthrop Rocketeller at a Rocketeller estate in New York.

Winthrop: Jacob, I hope you've been getting along ok, considering all of the recent troubles with Machiavelli Bank.

Jacob: It's been a struggle, even with the bailout. I had to sell one of my castles.

Winthrop (huffs): How unbearable!

Jacob: And now the nerve of those tax slaves, not paying their taxes! What is this world coming to?
Winthrop: Yes, Jacob, I know. But the good news is that once our plan to take over the digital currency market is complete, then things will then again be in our favor. (passes platter to Jacob) More truffle-infused pheasant?

Jacob (smug grin): Delightful. Yes, Winthrop, to keep the status quo intact, we can't waste any time. The central banks of the world can only finance governments for so long without adequate taxes. And, well, I don't want to even think about what might happen if our illusory authoritarian structures crumble.

Winthrop: Shudder at the thought. Speaking of which, do you have any idea if people are learning about Natural Law?

Jacob: I haven't been made aware of anything from our data collection agencies.

Winthrop: Neither have I, but this anti-tax movement has me worried. We'd better take a look and see if people are learning how to be free. If they are, then……

Jacob: Yes, I know. No more slaves. We'll have to actually produce something.

Winthrop: Anyway, let's talk about the task at hand. You're sure everything in Alaska is guarded well enough? We don't want any trouble from your bastard child, Bong.

Jacob: Virtually impenetrable. That place is crawling with order-followers. And if he does decide to show up, there's a little surprise waiting for him.

Winthrop: OOOO, a surprise? Like what? A killer robot penguin?

Jacob: No, not a killer robot penguin. Where do you come up with this stuff?

Scene 3

Bong has just landed his jet a couple miles from the military installation in Alaska. He's now trudging through the snow, wearing a military officer's uniform and carrying a briefcase.

K: Bong!

Bong (glances at smartwatch): I'm busy trudging right now, K. This better be important.

K: It is! I just wanted to let you know that I'm sitting in the warm sun while you're freezing.

Bong: I'm so elated.

K: And I thought you might wanna know that once you get close enough to a quantum machine, we might have communication problems.

Bong: I wasn't planning on calling you anyway.

K: Famous last words. Good luck, Bong.

A while later, and Bong is approaching a fence on the perimeter of the compound. He's approached by 2 machine gun clad thugs in uniforms.

Thug 1: This is a restricted area. Got some ID?

Bong: What, you mean a card?

Thug 2: Yeah, an ID card.

Bong (irritated): How antiquated is this operation? Wait until the Committee hears about this. Why aren't you using biometrics?

Thug 1: Well, we use biometrics inside.

Bong: Oh, ya do, huh?! That's going in my report.

Thug 2: Report? And what committee?

Bong: That's on a need to know basis. And address me as sir!

Thug 1: We still need to see your ID, sir.

Bong: Well, I don't have any 20th century ID with me, fellas. So if you don't want General Flounder to hear about this, I suggest ya let me pass before I get frostbite.

Thug 2: General who?

Bong (feigning shock): You don't know General Flounder? What's your name? You're going in my report.

Thug 1 and Thug 2 look at each other and shrug.

Thug 1: Ok, go ahead. What's your name, sir? I'll just put it in the log.

Bong: Colonel Ruse.

Thug 2: Ok, sir, thank you.

Bong makes his way to the main building, where he finds a large steel doorway controlled by iris scanners. He scans his eyes multiple times and is denied entrance. Soon, a weary-looking order-follower shows up in uniform.

Weary Order-follower: I'll need to…

Bong cuts him off.

Bong: You'll need to explain yourself! I'm not in the database yet?

Order-follower (confused): Um, who are you?

Bong: I'm Colonel Ruse. Who are you? Why hasn't the biometric database been updated yet?

Order-follower (bumbling): Well, sir, I, I….

Bong: Must be pretty brilliant if you can't remember your own name. (rolls eyes) It's freezing out here.

Order-follower: Yes, sir, please come in.

Bong steps into the dank, cavernous structure.

Bong (sigh of relief): Well, that's better. Point me in the direction of some hot chocolate and I won't put you in my report. I'll let you off with a warning.

Order-follower: Thank you, sir. Just down the hall, second right is the mess hall.

Bong continues and once the coast is clear, he starts searching for his target. He comes across a corridor that leads underground. Following this path, he soon comes to another guarded entrance. Two uniformed order-followers greet him.

Order-follower 1: Yes, sir. Can we help you?

Bong: I'm here writing a status report for General Flounder.

Order-follower 2: General who?

Bong (huffs): You don't know General Flounder? Shame. This is going in my report.

Order-follower 1: Hold on, now. There's no need to do that. It's just that we don't have anyone on our list for a scheduled visit.

Bong (offended): Oh, you don't! Who's in charge of communications at this facility?

Both order-followers have no idea, so they mumble incoherently.

Bong: Look, this is mission critical. (moves in close to whisper) We're on the verge of going to Code Indigo. I must speak with the lead science team at once.

Order-follower 2: Code Indigo? What's that?

Bong: You'll find out the hard way if I can't speak with that science team.

Order-follower 1: All right, I'll scan ya in.

He scans his eyes and the steel door slides open. Inside, there are four military guards, and a team of scientists. The scientists are performing various tasks. In the center of the room is the quantum computer, about the size of a washing machine. The room is noticeably warmer. Bong quickly pulls a thin silicon wafer that contains the nanobots from the briefcase. Just as he's about to release the nanobots, an elderly scientist approaches him with a guard.

Scientist: May I ask what you're doing?

Bong: We've gone to Code Indigo. You didn't get the memo?

Guard: Code Indigo?

Scientist: You look familiar. I know you from somewhere.

Bong: I don't think so. I get that a lot, actually. People say I look like one of the old James Bond characters. You know, those silly old spy movies.

Scientist: No, no wait. I never forget a face. I knew you from many years ago. I worked in the Super Soldier program. You're James Bong!

Bong pulls a gas canister from his pocket and releases the gas. It's super concentrated, aerosolized THC. Everyone is knocked out in seconds, including Bong.

End Episode 17

Episode 18

Scene 1

Acapulco at K's place….

K: Bong's down. His camera is still active. Are you live streaming this on Dlive, Moneybit?

Miss Moneybit: Yep, and Hollyweird ain't got nothin on this.

K (sarcastic): I'm glad that Bong's plight is good for your ratings.

Symphy: Bong has failed to activate the nanobots.

K: He hasn't failed….yet.

Back in Alaska….

Bong wakes up first, sees the unconscious bodies, and takes a moment to process the situation.

Bong (thinking to himself, groggy): Super-THC concentrate, a very refreshing way to temporarily neutralize enemies.

Bong goes to the quantum computer and activates nanobots. Then he leaves the compound and races towards his private jet a couple miles away. Upon reaching the jet, he's met by uniformed order-followers in all black uniforms. They raise weapons and laser sights appear all over Bong.

Bong: Good job, guys. The training drill is over!

Order-follower 1 (uncertain, talks to captain): Cap'n, what drill?

Captain Ringer: He's lying, obviously! Don't believe him for a second! (to Bong) Well, James Bong, it's been too long. You remember me, right?

Bong (squinting, thinking): Ah, yes, I remember. You're from that reality TV show, "Don't Let This Happen To You", right?

Order-followers chuckle.

Captain Ringer (to order-followers): Enough! (to Bong) Well, same old Bong. (gets close to Bong's face) Russia? 2024?

Bong: Oh, Captain Ringer, yes! Now I remember! One of the most bloodthirsty devils on the planet. I didn't recognize you in the all black uniform. Does your little patch there say "Murder, Inc."? Is that Blackwater's new name?

Captain Ringer: Real funny, coming from you, Bong. You're no saint. You were in the war.

Bong: But I learned from my mistakes and now I atone for my sins.

Order-follower 1: Cap'n, it's cold! Can we get goin?

Captain Ringer: Damnit, how did you make it through basic?! (to Bong) You missed out, Bong. Private security is where the money is.

Bong: You mean private mercenary. So what are you gonna do with me, Ringer?

Captain Ringer: I should kill you.

Bong: You want to, but you won't.

Captain Ringer: Why is that?

Bong (bold): Because you're an order-follower, and you're afraid of what the order-givers might do to you if you make a mistake.

Captain Ringer (deep breath): Bong, I will keep you alive, for now. You're probably worth more that way to some very powerful people.

Scene 2

Back inside the military compound in Alaska, Bong is cuffed and inside an electric-bar holding cell. Various workers of the compound are plotting near him.

Bong: Fancy cell, huh?

Order-follower 1: The base commander is off duty, Cap'n.

Captain Ringer: It's very important, so I'm sure he won't mind being bothered on his off time.

Scientist: Whatever you do, do it fast. Mr. Bong has sabotaged our mission with nanobots in the quantum computer.

Bong: Can't you think of a catchy nickname for that thing? I mean, quantum computer is so dry and practical. How about "Big Q?".

Scientist: You still don't recognize me, Bong?

Captain Ringer (to scientist): You know him, Doctor Slashdemeind?

Dr. Slashdemeind: Yes, we go way back. But no time to reminisce. We've got to disable the nanobots.

Order-follower 2: Cap'n, the base commander is on the line for you. Should I put it on speaker?
Captain Ringer (facepalm): No. (to commander on phone) Sir, we've captured James Bong. What are your orders?

Commander: Hell if I know! Damnit, why does stuff like this happen on my day off? I'll have to contact Washington to see what their orders are.

Captain Ringer: Yes, sir.

Bong starts laughing.

Captain Ringer: What now, Bong?

Bong: None of you can make a decision yourselves! It's funny, in a sad and pathetic way.

Scene 3

General Small is napping at his desk at CIA headquarters. He's startled awake by a blaring ringtone.

General Small (mumbling to self): Still can't get that damn ringer fixed. (answers call) Small, here.

Base Commander: General Small, this is Commander Twitzel. We've captured James Bong in a sabotage operation. What are your orders?

General Small: I order you to await the orders I get from my boss.

Twitzel: Understood, sir. Twitzel out.

Meanwhile back in Alaska, Captain Ringer is pacing around, waiting for orders. The other rights-violators are playing poker with hover cards.

Bong: How long does it take to make a decision in your immoral, hellish little hierarchy?

Ringer (yelling at other order-followers): Someone muzzle him!

Doctor Slashdemeind: I have an idea that might make everybody happy. Well, everybody here except Bong.

Ringer: I'm listening.

Slashdemeind: If you will allow it, I can make some adjustments to Mr. Bong.

Ringer: Adjustments?

Slashdemeind: Yes, a simple brain implant. Not only will it be traceable so that Bong might lead us to his associates, but it serves another purpose as well. We can torture him remotely, if necessary, to gain compliance.

Ringer: Great idea, but I can't authorize that. It'll have to wait.

And in London, Sir Hugo Trax is doing air golf swings in his office at MI6, when his holo-phone alerts him to a call.

Trax: This better be good. I'm swamped!

Small: Trax, it's Small! Bong has been captured trying to sabotage operation Q-money! Should we have him killed?

Trax: No, fool! Don't do anything until I talk to Gateschild!

Small: Yes, sir.

In Davos, Switzerland, Jacob Gateschild is having a business meeting with some bankster associates. He's gloating about how soon the cryptocurrency market will be cornered. One of his assistants franticlally scurries into the meeting room and whispers into Jacob's ear.

Jacob Gateschild: What?! Are you sure? (more whispering from assistant) Excuse me, gentlemen, I'll be right back.

Gateschild steps out and makes a call to Sir Hugo Trax.

Gateschild: Mr. Trax, what have you done!?

Trax: I haven't done anything, sir.

Gateschild: Precisely! You've allowed Bong to interfere once again!

Trax: That's why I contacted you, sir. What should we do?

Gateschild: Oh, for Satan's sake, that's your job, Trax. Figure it out! What the hell do I pay you for?!

Click.

Scene 4

The next morning. After many more calls down the chain of command, it finally got back to Captain Ringer. The order was, basically, handle it, Ringer! So Ringer agreed to Doctor Slashdemeind's idea to put an implant in Bong's brain. Slashdemeind is preparing the necessary tools and gadgets for the surgery.

Meanwhile, in Acapulco….

K (frantically hacking away on keyboard): Symphy, we gonna make it in time?

Symphy: Due to the illogical nature of human actions, especially those in rigid authoritarian hierarchies, it is difficult to make an accurate calculation.

Miss Moneybit (sarcastic): Come on, Symphy, where's that robot intuition?

Symphy: I do not possess what you call intuition.

K: She was joking, Symphy.

Symphy: Once again, humor puzzles me.

Back in Alaska….

Captain Ringer (speaking to Bong through the electric cell bars): Bong! Time for surgery. Chop chop!

Bong: I can't have surgery before my morning coffee.

Captain Ringer: Maybe I can have the good doctor do something about that distorted sense of humor of yours.

They enter what Slashenmeind has turned into a makeshift operating room. Bong is laid onto a table and strapped down.

Meanwhile, a fleet of drones, ranging in size from a mosquito to a laptop computer are approaching the military installation. One of the drones is searching for the correct frequency to knock out power to the compound. Others seek out the armed guards and knock them out with ultra THC-tipped darts. Yet another finds a way to hack the door locks and allow entry.

Slashenmeind: Captain Ringer, I do believe electricity will be necessary for me to complete this operation.

Ringer: Damnit, is Bong's sarcasm rubbing off on you? I'll make a call and see what the hell is going on.

The drones methodically and efficiently make their way towards where Bong is being held, incapacitating order-followers with THC-tipped darts as necessary. Once inside the operating room, they allow the power to be reactivated. Slashenmeind and Ringer freeze from being caught off guard, and are easily incapacitated with the THC darts. One of the drones cuts Bong loose, and he flees on foot with a multi-drone escort. Bong gets into his private jet and flies off.

The next day in Acapulco….

Bong: Sure took you long enough to show up.

K: Well, if they would've gotten that chip in you, then they might have found out my location. I couldn't let that happen.

Miss Moneybit: Will you two get over yourselves? I just ate.

Bong: Did all the trouble have our desired outcome, I hope?

K: Yeah, there have already been significant changes in the market. The best part is, since so many people watched it live on Moneybit's Dlive feed, the 3 coins controlled by the banksters plummeted within minutes of you disabling their quantum fraud machine.

Bong: I wish I could've seen the look on old Gateschild's face.

K: Hmmmmm…..

Moneybit: Don't give K any ideas.

End Episode 18

Episode 19

Scene 1

At K's place in Acapulco, K is hacking away on multiple keyboards with Symphy, and Bong is just finishing up his morning workout with sit-ups.

Bong (finished): And 250.

K: Show off.

Bong: Have you ever done a sit-up?

K: Nope. No need, I'm naturally chiseled.

Bong: I'm not sure chiseled is quite the correct word for your physique. Have you ever tried to do a sit-up?

K: Well, no, not really.

Miss Moneybit bursts energetically onto the scene.

K: Hey, whatever happened to knocking?

Moneybit (sarcastic): I thought our relationship was past that.

Bong: Your timing is impeccable, actually. K was just about to do one sit-up.

Moneybit (rolls eyes): Right. Anyway, I'm so excited! I was just contacted by Elon Shiller!

K: The super-eccentric Ancap billionaire?

Moneybit: Yep! You know how he's been building an independent seasteading community infrastructure?

Bong and K look at each other and shrug.

Moneybit (hands on hips); I told you guys about this over a year ago!

Bong (cringing): Ah, yes, sure, I remember now.

Moneybit: Sure ya do….Anyway, he's invited me to take a personal tour of the whole project! And I can bring whoever I want!

K: Wow! Cool, so who's going with you?

Moneybit: You two!

K: Really? Why?

Moneybit: I have no idea.

K: That's very generous, but I can't leave the lair.

Moneybit: You're joking.

Bong: He's not joking. When was the last time you left the lair, K?

K: You don't really expect me to remember that, do you?

Moneybit looks off into the distance, and appears to be contemplating something disturbing.

Bong: Moneybit, you ok?

Moneybit: Yeah, just wondering how many wrong turns I made to end up with you two as my top picks to go on this trip. (sighs) So you're both coming, right?

K: I dunno, maybe.

Moneybit: Come on! It's a technological marvel!

K (excited): It is! Why didn't ya say so?

Moneybit: I thought it was painstakingly obvious.

K: I'm in! Bong?

Bong (reluctant): I'll go. But not because I think I'll enjoy it. Just simply to watch your back.

Moneybit: Awww, that's sweet, James.

Bong: Well, honestly, I was more concerned with K. I know you can handle yourself, Moneybit.

Scene 2

The next day, K, Moneybit, and Bong are on the verge of leaving K's lair. Moneybit and Bong are standing by the front door with Symphy. There is a large stack of assorted luggage leaning against the wall.

Bong: Moneybit, is all this really necessary? It's only one weekend.

Moneybit: Yeah, that's why I've only got one small bag.

Bong: You mean all this is K's?

K scurries in, wearing oversized shades, a fedora, baggy cargo shorts, and a Hawaiian shirt buttoned all the way to the top. He's also carrying an umbrella.

131

K: Ok, let's roll!

Bong: K, are you relocating? What's with all the bags?

K: Just the essentials. Can you start loading it in the seaplane for me?

Bong: If you can't carry it yourself, you can't bring it. And what's with the umbrella? There isn't a cloud in the sky.

K: It's a sunbrella, thank you very much. I've gotta gradually ease my way back into the sun.

Moneybit: Please don't embarrass me in front of Mr. Shiller.

Bong: That's a tall order for our friend, Mr. K.

K (to Symphy): Symphy, this is your first time being alone. Take good care of the lair.

Symphy: Yes, K.

K: Don't forget to run the maintenance on the holo-imager.

Symphy: Yes, K.

K: And the keyboards are due for a good dusting.

Symphy: Yes, K.

Moneybit: Symphy, if you find him annoying, feel free to make a snide remark.

Symphy: I am not programmed to make snide remarks.

Moneybit: Want me to do it for you?

Symphy (smiling): That is a nice gesture, Miss Moneybit. Thank you.

Scene 3

Bong has just landed the seaplane near the vast seasteading project of Elon Shiller. An automated walkway extends itself from a large floating platform to the seaplane. As the three make their way down the walkway, an energetic Elon Shiller is waving hello and yelling greetings from the platform.

Bong (whispering to moneybit): Eccentric and flamboyant, looks like.

Moneybit: The yin to your yang.

Bong: I do just fine without yin, thanks.

Elon rushes in and hugs Moneybit.

Elon: A pleasure to meet you, darling! (looks at Bong) And let me guess...this is the undeniable Mr. Bong! (holds out hand, Bong reluctantly shakes, then Elon turns to K) And who's this?

K (flamboyant): The indestructible Mr. K.

Bong: He doesn't get out much.

Elon (motioning towards the entrance to what appears to be a huge suacer-shaped ship) Please, let's have lunch and I'll tell you all you want to know about the first free, autonomous human settlement on earth!

Scene 4

Bong and Co. are having lunch with Elon Shiller in an underwater dining room.

Bong: So you say that there will be no external government here, is that right?

Shiller: Exactly! Only internal government! Only one law, that is, Natural Law! And I expect that many others will be pursuing similar aims in the near future, Mr. Bong. And I want you and Miss Moneybit to be a part of it! At the very least, give some street cred in the anarchist community, for lack of a better term.

K (wipes mouth with forearm): This is delicious, by the way. So you're going to live here?

Shiller: Most of the time, yes.

Moneybit: How many "houses" do you have to sell?

Shiller: Ten right now, and they're already sold. Most of them are my friends, and others passed the test.

Bong: Test?

Shiller: Yes, a one question test. They have to tell me the definition of a "wrong".

K: Clever. Will you have internet?

Shiller: No, we'll be in the stone ages.....just kidding. Yes, of course!

Bong: Have you had any trouble with the government gang?

Shiller (face sours slightly, hesitates): No, no, none of any significance to speak of.

K: What about electricity?

Shiller: Right now, mostly Ocean Thermal Nano Conversion, which also helps desalinize the water, by the way. Two birds, one stone, that sort of deal. (grins)

133

Moneybit: What about food? Will you ship it all in?

Shiller (scoffs): Heavens no! I've already got enough aquaculture to be self-sufficient and will soon have enough to trade. But I don't want to bore you all with the nuts and bolts of the operation! Let me give you the tour! See for yourself!

Shiller guides them around the vast budding small town. Various bubble and sub shaped houses and other "buildings" for utility and recreation, all located at varying depths. While on the tour, Bong repeatedly spots tiny circular dots fixed high on the walls. Bong considers asking what purpose they serve, but decides it might be better to research the matter later, so he takes 3D photos with his smartwatch.

Scene 5

After a weekend of wining and dining, Bong, K, and Moneybit return to K's place in Acapulco. K is the color of a deep red lobster from head to toe.

Symphy: Welcome home.

K: Thanks Symphy, I'm never going out again.

Bong (huffs): Poor Symphy.

Moneybit: So that was awesome, right, guys? I'm gonna do a full report on it on dtube.

Bong: I love the concept, but I can't commit to endorsing it just yet.

Moneybit: Why, what's wrong?

Bong: I've got to look into it further.

Moneybit (narrows eyes): Hmmm, Bong, what are you up to? What's the deal?

Bong: Probably nothing. (turns to Symphy) Symphy, might I have a word?

K: What about me? You need my help?

Bong: Symphy will do just fine. Go take an aloe bath or something. You're painful just to look at.

Moneybit: K's bathing, that's my cue to leave. (Moneybit walks out)

Bong and Symphy go into the main core of K's hacker lair. K trails gingerly behind.

Bong (sarcastic): Don't trust me alone with your robot?

K: I just don't want an amateur like you messing up any of the equipment in my lair.

Bong loads photos into the holo-projector.

Bong: Symphy, do you recognize this?

Symphy: It appears to be some type of human dwelling.

K: You have to be more specific, Bong.

Bong: Right. (zooms in on the circular object on the wall in question) This. Do you know its function or its composition?

Symphy: It is not an apparatus that I am familiar with. I am analyzing for content and practical usage. One moment.

K: What are you getting at, Bong?

Bong: It might be nothing, but I noticed something when I asked him about government gang interference. His demeanor changed. He hesitated. And then I noticed hundreds of these tiny devices attached to the walls of every structure in the complex.

Symphy: Analysis complete. It appears to be a synthetic multi-functional nano-material.

Bong: In English?

K: It's a nano-material that can serve multiple functions simultaneously, but with the added twist that it's programmed to change into other functions on command. It's been rumored to exist, but not proven.

Bong: Until now. Symphy, do you know the functions?

Symphy: It appears to have 3 functions. Energy conduit, air pressure monitor, and data collection.

Bong: Data collection? What kind of data collection?

Symphy: Video, audio, and meta are all confirmed.

Bong: Is there one not confirmed?

Symphy: I speculate that gathering of cognitive data is also done with this device.

Bong and K share a wide-eyed look.
K: Not a true anarchist, looks like.

Bong: That's an understatement. Symphy, can you speculate on other nano-functions that are not currently operating?

Symphy: Based on all available data, there could theoretically be 888 more functions for this device.

Bong: How many that could be used to harm others?
Symphy: Theoretically, twenty could be used to intentionally harm humans.

K: Twenty!
Bong gets up to leave.

K: Where are you going?
Bong: To play 20 questions with Mr. Shiller.

End Episode 19

Episode 20

Scene 1

Bong has just arrived at Elon Shiller's seasteading community project once again. Shiller is having a holo-video conference when he is alerted by his security system that there is an unexpected visitor.

Shiller: Bong is here. We'll have to continue later. Bye.

Shiller takes deep breath and goes to meet Bong at the main entry port.

Shiller: Mr. Bong! Back so soon! What a pleasant surprise!

Bong: We need to have a chat in private.

Shiller: I'd be delighted! Let's have a drink in the undersea lounge.

Bong: Thanks, but I think we should talk on my seaplane. A bit more private, if you don't mind.

Shiller: Mr. Bong, this is a state-of-the-art facility! I guarantee it has the highest security protocols available.

Bong: I must insist otherwise.

Shiller: Very well. You can show me some of those fancy pilot tricks they must teach you at MI6.

Bong and Shiller board Bong's hemp-powered seaplane and zoom off.

Shiller: So have you decided to endorse my project? It'll….

Bong cuts him off.

Bong: Take a look at this.

A holographic image of one of the nano-transmitters pops up in front of them.

Bong: Care to explain what that is?

Shiller gets stunned look.

Bong: Lost for words? Let me have a crack at it. Spy tech that's ubiquitous throughout your seasteading infrastructure, capable of reading thoughts. Not exactly what a true voluntarist would do.

Shiller: Look, Bong…

Bong cuts him off.

Bong: I'm not finished. Not only that, but the nano-particles in these devices also have explosive capabilities. Is that a quaint little self-destruct feature you built in and decided to keep secret?

Shiller: Bong, I know what this must look like. I didn't want to have that system installed, but I had no choice.

Bong (incredulous sarcasm): No choice? Well, that's awfully ripe, now isn't it? You didn't have any choice to rig your own multi-million dollar project with explosives?

Shiller: Lemme explain. They threatened my wife and my children if I didn't comply. I had to do it to save them!

Bong: Who's they?

Shiller: I never saw his face! He said he was representing some "concerned individuals". He knew things about my family that nobody knows. Nobody! And he knew things about me, too. What was I supposed to do?

Bong: Anything but lure innocent people into living in a ticking time bomb, that's what.

Shiller: Look, James, maybe I should've done things differently, but it's not too late! Maybe you could help me.

Bong: And why should I do that?

Shiller: Because it's an opportunity to start a real, voluntary community! Only one law! The Golden Rule! That's why you came here on your first visit, right? If you can help me protect my family, I'd gladly get rid of that system.

Bong: You and your family can't hide forever. At some point you'll have to take responsibility and face your fears.

Shiller: Yeah, I know that. But in the short term, my family would need to be secreted away somehow to buy me some time.

Bong: I'll consider it. In the meantime, don't expect any glowing reviews for your project from Miss Moneybit's Dtube channel.

Shiller: I figured as much.

Scene 2

In Acapulco, K is jamming out to some 70s funk music while he and Symphy are researching Elon Shiller. After finding some alarming information, he calls Bong's encrypted smartwatch.

K: Bong!

Bong: What now, K?

K: Symphy and I did some digging into Elon Shiller.

Bong: And?

K: It looks like he's a shill. You wouldn't believe what we found.

Bong: Try me. And what's that noise?

K: You mean the funk?

Bong: Yes, the funk. Please stop the funk.

K: Bong, just so ya know, the funk can't be stopped. I'll turn it down, though. So anyway, Shiller didn't exactly pull himself up by the bootstraps as some daring entrepreneur, like the media makes him out to be. Nearly all of his companies are shells within shells, a paper trail that would normally be impossible to follow, but Symphy is anything but normal.

Bong: Can you gloat about the A.I. robot you created later, and just get to the point?

K: Bottom line is, nearly all of his financing has come from oligarch-owned banks. He's a front man, Bong.

Bong: A shill, and a dangerous one. An anarchist in name only, not in practice. If a bunch of true, peaceful anarchists were to move to his seasteading community.....

K: And there would be a violent explosion.

Bong: It would be a propagandist's dream scenario to paint anarchy in a bad light and try to put the lid on the awakening that's been happening. So much for Shiller's sob story about his family being in danger.

K: Oh, and I almost forgot, check this out. Guess who's financing a so-called smart city on the sea? The Gateschilds, fresh off their bailout for Machiavelli Bank.

Bong: Naturally. Good work, K. Have Moneybit meet me at your place. I'll be there in an hour.

Scene 3

Sir Hugo Trax is sitting with his feet up on his desk at MI6, when he receives a holo-call.

Sir Hugo Trax (mumbling to himself, eyeing the clock): They just have to call right when it's about time to knock off for the day.

Answers call. Elon Shiller's face pops up above Trax's desk.

Trax: Shiller, it's almost beer thirty, so make it quick.

Shiller: Bong knows.

Trax: Bong knows what?

Shiller: He found the nano-devices.

Trax: And what'd you tell him?

Shiller: I gave him some sob story about how my family was threatened and forced to install the devices. So what now?

Trax ponders for a moment.

Trax: Well, we could run a fake news story about your family being kidnapped.

Shiller (adamant): I think not.

Trax: Or we could actually kidnap your family.

Shiller: Not funny.

Trax: I wasn't joking.

Shiller: You're not helping.

Trax: Look, just hang tight and I'll figure something out.

Click.

Scene 4

Bong, Miss Moneybit, K, and Symphy are meeting at K's place.

Moneybit: Glad I didn't put out a promo video for that Shill community. The nerve!

K: So Bong, you got your conversation with Shiller recorded, right?

Bong: No, the batteries died.

K: What?!

Bong: You're far too gullible. Yes, of course it's recorded.

K: Great, so we have evidence that Shiller's seasteading community is compromised.

Bong: And you've got data to show that Shiller is actually a front man for the Gateschilds. Moneybit, that's enough to make a solid report, right?

Moneybit: I'll have it up on Dtube tomorrow.

Scene 5

The next day at K's place.....

Symphy: K, there is a news story on BNN which I think you'll find relevant to the Shiller situation.

K (yawning on couch): Oh yeah, what's that?

Symphy: Shiller is reported to be dead.

K (jumps up): What?! Lemme see!

A hologram pops up in the middle of K's techno-lair with a BNN news feed:
Elon Shiller is believed to be dead after an explosion destroyed his latest brainchild, a high-tech seasteading community off the Pacific Coast near Cabo San Lucas. While it's not yet confirmed, it is believed that the attack was carried out by the infamous anarchist James Bong, along with other members of his gang, a female conspiracy theorist known as Miss Moneybit and a male hacker known only as K. BNN has obtained original video footage of the three just days ago visiting the multi-million dollar project spearheaded by Shiller.

K: Man, just my luck. My first time out of the house in years, and then this?

Symphy: Your priorities confuse me.

K: It was dark sarcasm, to lighten my mood. I gotta talk to Bong and Moneybit!

K dials up a conference call on the holo-phone.

K: Moneybit! Did you put that report on Shiller out yet?

Moneybit: No, it's only 8am. I am human, ya know.

K: Turn on BNN!

Bong and Moneybit both check out the report.

Bong: How convenient.

Moneybit: Guess I'd better hold off.

Bong: Yeah, but not as long as you might think. I smell a rat.

K: What do you mean?

Bong: I fancy a flight right now. Don't publish anything yet.

Scene 6

Bong is flying near the seasteading site, which is perfectly intact. Bong dials up K and Moneybit on his smart watch.

Bong: Do you see what I see?

Moneybit: The control panel in your jet?

Bong (repositioning camera): Sorry, bad angle. Now?

K: Is that what I think it is?

Bong: If you think it's a multi-million dollar seasteading complex that has not been blown to smitherines, then you are correct. I think you might want to file this in your report, Moneybit.

Moneybit (sighs): The info war just went to another level.

End Episode 20

142

Episode 21

Scene 1

General Small is in his office at CIA headquarters. He's about to dig into a mega-large pizza when he gets a call on his holo-phone.

Mr. Hack: Sir, this is Hack, from data analytics.

Small: Kinda busy right now with this giant pizza, but go ahead.

Mr Hack: Sorry, sir, but it's urgent. I've noticed an alarming trend in fictional writings and videos with themes of anarchy. They're becoming quite popular at an exponential rate.

Small (rolling eyes): Ok, Mr. Hack, I'll make a note of that. Anything else?

Mr. Hack: With all due respect, sir, you do realize that the control of popular fiction has been an indispensible cornerstone of all big governments throughout history.

Small (condescending): Look, this isn't really my department, but I'll pass it on up the old command channels, ok?

Click.

Starts to take a bite of pizza when his holo-phone rings with a call from his boss Sir Hugo Trax at MI6.

Small (annoyed): Trax, I'm about to have pizza. Can you call me back in 20?

Sir Hugo Trax: Small, the world doesn't revolve around your feeding schedule.

Small: Well, maybe it should.

Trax: I've come up with a fool-proof plan to finally get to Bong, and I need you to get it implemented immediately.

Small: If it's so fool proof, why don't you do it yourself?

Trax: Cuz if it fails, I can blame you. That's what I love about hierarchies.

Small (sighs): The things I do for a pension. Ok, lay it on me.

Trax: It involves Operation Nanobrain.

Small: You're not really going to risk that op are you? And who thinks of these ludicrous names, anyhow?

143

Trax: Just don't screw it up, Small, and the op will continue as normal. And then we can get Bong out of the way and maybe stem the tide of this trend in anarchist thought. I've seen far too many "taxation is theft" t-shirts the past few weeks.

Small: Yeah, so what's the big deal about a few t-shirts?

Trax (facepalm): Small, I'm sure you're aware of the growing number of people refusing to pay taxes here and in the US. You do realize that without taxes, there goes your pension.

Small (gasps): This is cause for alarm! Ok, Trax, your scare tactics worked. Oh yeah, and that reminds me of something I was supposed to tell you, something from a call I just got from analytics. Hmmm......(shrugs) Oh, well, can't be that important. I might remember later. So what's your fool-proof plan?

Scene 2

At K's place in Acapulco, K is playing Pac-Man with Symphy and listening to 80s synth. K is losing badly.

Symphy: If you would like, I can downgrade my ability settings to make it a more enjoyable competition for you.

K (defiant): Nope, I'll beat you eventually. It's only a matter of time.

Symphy: The human life span does not allow for such possibilities.

K (sighs): Very funny.

Symphy: There is an encrypted message from an unknown source coming in.

K: Ok, pause Pac-Man and throw it up on the holo-screen.

K reads the message. It's from a scientist who claims to be a whistleblower at a secret research project in China.

K: Hmm, interesting. Symphy, check out his credentials and let me know if you think it's legit.

Symphy: Yes, K.

Scene 3

A few hours later, Bong is sipping red wine on a beach in Chile when he gets a call on his encrypted smart watch.

K: Bong!

Bong: What now, K?

K: You're going to China! Congratulations.

Bong: Oh, am I? And why is that?

K: I've got a hankerin for some authentic Chinese cuisine.

Bong: K!

K: Ok, ok. I got some encrypted messages from a scientist who wants to blow the whistle on a project he says he's involved with in China. According to his file photo, his name is Dr. Bill Spiller. Symphy and I checked out the details he gave us, and it looks like they check out. Harvard and MIT big shot....

Bong cuts him off.

Bong: Just skip to the important stuff. I don't need to hear how many hoops he jumped through.

K: You know about DNA computers?

Bong: Yeah.

K: Well, he invented it.

Bong (sarcastic): All by himself just tinkering in a garage somewhere, I imagine.

K: Ok, he was on a team that developed it, anyway. He's worked for some heavy hitters in the past, like Lockheed-Boeing and DARPA.

Bong: Who's he with now?

K: That's the thing, I couldn't find his current status. He didn't say the company name or the project. However, in the message I got from him, and this was heavily encrypted so I'm not certain this is correct, Symphy thinks it's involving the Falun Gong. You know about that group, right?

Bong: Yes, they're highly repressed in China and targeted for organ harvesting. What would a guy like Spiller be doing there?

K: Or his employers, for that matter.

Bong: And a way to contact him? Or shall I just send smoke signals?

K: He gave me coordinates.

Bong (takes final gulp of wine): How about you go this time, and I'll sip Chilean wine.

K: I have a better idea! Before you go to China, you can make a pit stop here and drop off a fine Chilean wine for me.

Bong: Are you hallucinating?

K: Oh, come on, why not? You afraid of getting stopped by the uniformed extortion-funded pirates, also known as customs?

Bong (scoffs): Don't insult my ego to get what you want. You know I fly under the radar.

K: Bring a bottle for Miss Moneybit, too!

Bong: Goodbye, K.

Click.

Scene 4

2 days later. Longmen Mountains west of Chengdu, China. Bong has just landed his 3D printed plane, modeled after the Beechcraft King Air 350i. He's on foot, approaching the designated coordinates where he is to meet Dr. Spiller. Bong calls K on his smartwatch.

K: Bong! You never showed up with the wine.

Bong: You seem to whine enough, so I thought better of it. Look, I'm within about a half a kilometer of the coordinates you gave me. There's nothing here that I can see, at least above ground. Go ahead and signal him.

K: Got it. Oh, and your video feed from your shoulder cam isn't so hot.

Bong (annoyed): Perhaps you can get around to fixing that while you're lounging around Acapulco. In the meantime, I'm gonna try and do my job here on the ground.

K: So testy. Jet lag?

Bong hangs up. Within a few minutes, an ATV appears on the horizon and makes its way towards Bong. A tall, thin, nervous looking character gets out and meets Bong.

Bong: Dr. Spiller?

Spiller: Mr. Bong. Are you recording?

Bong: Of course.

Spiller: For my protection, I must insist on no recording.

Bong: For your protection and mine, I must insist on documenting everything here. Otherwise, I'll do a little mountain hiking, and be on my way. Good luck getting your story out through any of the oligarch-owned propaganda channels.

Spiller: Very well, Mr. Bong. You leave me little choice.

Bong: Who do you work for?

146

Spiller: I can't say. What I can tell you is what I know of the project, and where you can verify, if you wish.

Bong: You mentioned Falun Gong in your message.

Spiller: Yes, they are our test subjects.

Bong: Does this involve organ harvesting?

Spiller: Certain members of the Chinese elite are concerned with that, but that's not why I contacted you.

Bong: When you say "elite", you mean the ruling psychopaths in corporations and government? And you don't have a problem with violently stealing someone's organs and their life? Not to mention that organizations you worked for in the past, like Lockheed-Boeing, were extortion-funded merchants of death?

Spiller: I'm not here to debate morals with you, Mr. Bong. Besides, that is only a subproject of what goes on where I work. The main objective of the operation is, at least I thought, develop more efficient and practical uses for DNA computers. But there is a dark agenda afoot in the use of that technology.

Bong: Darker than murdering and stealing organs?

Spiller: We were recently teamed up with a pharmaceutical company and tasked with finding a way to make DNA computing transferable via a vaccine.

Bong: I see. One question about the ability of such technology. Does it have input and output?

Spiller: Yes.

Bong: So whoever has this DNA in them, will no longer have the ability to be autonomous? And I imagine your fear is that this will be done covertly by means of a vaccine?

Spiller: And that's why we're having this conversation.

Bong: What happens to the test subjects? Where do they live? How long do they keep the DNA in them?

Spiller: They're sent back out into the world to go on about their lives. We track them constantly, of course, to monitor how they behave in society. Their memories of being kidnapped and experimented on are erased, of course. Mr. Bong, that's all I can tell you to get you started. I'm arranging to leave within the week. Can you assure me that you won't go public with this until I've managed to flee?

Bong: One week.

Spiller: However, if you wish to gather more intel, I'm willing to give you the location of the base. I can't take you there myself, for obvious reasons.

Bong: Very well, Dr. Spiller.

Spiller: I'll send them to your associate immediately.

Bong extends hand and shakes with Spiller.

Bong: Good luck, Dr. Spiller.

Spiller rides away in his ATV. Bong starts walking back to his plane and calls K.

K: Bong, your timing is impeccable. I was just about to finally beat Symphy's high score on Pac-Man.

Bong (cringing): Glad your priorities are in line. Wouldn't want you watching the live feed I'm sending you or anything. Anyway, I need you to do more digging on Dr. Spiller. I put a microdot tracker in his hand, so let me know where he ends up. He's also sending you location data for what he says is the project base.

K: I don't get it. Why the tracker?

Bong: Cuz I don't buy his story. I have serious doubts that a veteran of highly immoral operations and with ties to various extortion-funded entities would suddenly have any moral qualms. And he didn't want to give any names at all. There's something else going on.

K: Gotcha. You're gonna try and get into the base? To what end?

Bong: To shut this operation down and free the Falun Gong.

End Episode 21

Episode 22

Scene 1

Bong has flown deeper into the mountains and set up a campsite. He is preparing to send a Hawk Drone to gather more information on the operation described to him by Dr. Bill Spiller. Then comes a call on his smartwatch from K.

K: Bong!

A holographic image of K's face pops up over Bong's campfire.

Bong: Tell me some news, K.

Miss Moneybit: Hi Bong!

K: News? Well, Miss Moneybit just got back from the beach.

Bong (sighs): That's nice. I just finished eating homemade popsicles on this blasted cold mountain. Could you please tell me what you found on Spiller's location?

Moneybit: Bong, is that a campfire? You don't have any smart thermals with you?

Bong: Call me old fashioned.

K: So we found out more about the so-called whistleblower, Dr. Spiller. Symphy checked the time stamps on the bio info we had previously found on him. It turns out it's just a few days old.

Bong: What a coincidence.

Moneybit (sarcastic): Bong the coincidence theorist!

K: So Symphy did a facial recognition search through internet archives and found his real name. The guy you met is Dr. Hector Helix.

Bong: So did he actually invent the DNA computer or not?

K: Yes and no. Ya see, he was on the development team with the real Dr. Spiller. But Dr. Spiller died in a car crash.

Bong: So it looks like some people are going through a lot of trouble to muddy the waters. So where did Helix go? And what are those coordinates he sent you?

K: The satellite imagery suggests that the coordinates he gave are some type of prison. (sarcastic) That was great of him to invite you!

Bong: I'll send a thank you card and flowers.

K: But the spot Helix went to is a couple miles away from the coordinates he gave you. The thing is, we couldn't find any data on his location. It's completely dark, as if it didn't exist.

Bong: Which means that's where we need to be to find out exactly what's going on here.
K: You sending that hawk drone that I see behind you? Why not a bong shaped drone instead?

Bong: I was going to send a bong shaped drone with a caricature of Miss Moneybit engraved on it, but didn't have time to get it done.

Moneybit: That would've been real subtle. Nice thinkin, Bong.

Scene 2

Dr. Helix is having a holo-video call with General Small.

General Small: So Bong hasn't showed up yet?

Dr. Helix (annoyed): No, not to my knowledge. And can't you just speak directly with the head of security? I'm in RnD, so what the hell are you asking me for? I did what you asked, giving bait to Bong.

General Small: Compartmentalization! The key to any authoritarian hierarchy. That's why!

Dr. Helix: And why don't you just leave Bong alone? The more you provoke him, the more he'll fight back. Haven't you figured that out yet?

General Small: Are you a Bong sympathizer?!

Dr. Helix: I don't have time for this. I have a deadline to meet. Don't worry, if Bong turns up, you'll hear about it, I'm sure, one way or another. (Helix reaches for call disconnect button)

General Small: Just what is that supposed to mean?

Click.

Meanwhile, the hawk drone that Bong sent is gathering intel, flying near the ghost facility where Helix works and drops a spider drone into the ventilation system. It then heads to the prison complex a couple miles away, where it also sends a spider drone into the vents.

Truckloads of prisoners are moved from the prison to Helix's facility, where they are run through a battery of psychological and physical tests. Some receive injections, some don't. There are massive warehouses full of vaccines that look ready to ship. Part of the ghost facility has surgical centers where organs are harvested. There are various order-followers in uniforms with the Chinese national cult symbol, as well as private rights-violating mercenaries dressed in all black tactical gear.

The prison itself is mammoth, housing thousands of prisoners behind bullet proof double paned glass. Bong has the hawk drop a crypto-bug on one of the facility's data transmission lines.

Scene 3

Bong has another holo-call with K.

Bong: K, how long until you can get in their systems with that bug I dropped?

K: With Symphy's help, hopefully within the hour. Why don't you go ahead and get out of there? We have enough data to bust this thing open and expose it online.

Bong: And just leave thousands of prisoners here? I don't think so.

K: You're going in?
Bong: With your help.

K (slurps coffee nonchalantly): Makin me work overtime today.

Bong (punching on a touchpad): I'm sending you coordinates. Send a second transport there.

K: For thousands of people? An airbus that size doesn't exist.

Bong: The transport is for me, K. Obviously I don't expect to single handedly help thousands of people flee. Fly my original plane out remotely if you can. It'll at least serve as a good diversion.

K: Got it. How about a mountain llama?

Bong: Yes, a bullet proof mountain llama that flies. How about that?

K: Come on, Bong. Get real. So how are you getting in?

Bong: I need you to blind their cameras on the perimeter.

K: I'll be creative.

Bong: I'm sure you will. One more thing. Send the resonance frequency for bullet proof double paned glass to my frequency generator.

Scene 4

A few order-following mercenaries are sitting around in a surveillance control room at the prison complex. The wall is filled with various live surveillance camera feeds. Suddenly, the feeds from the perimeter fence change. A music video of "Karma Chameleon" by Culture Club takes over the screens and plays at full volume.

Merc 1: Ahhhh! What the hell is this?!

Merc 2: It appears to be bad 80s pop music, sir!

Merc 1: I know damn well it's bad 80s pop music! What is it doing on the perimeter security feed!? Sound the alarm!

Meanwhile, Bong, dressed in 3D printed, all black tactical gear with lots of gaudy pins and medals dangling from his sleeve and chest, slices the barbed-wire perimeter fence open with a laser cutter. He dashes up to one of the emergency exits of the nearest building, where he finds a uniformed criminal having a smoke.

Bong: Don't you hear that alarm!? Don't you know what that means?! And you're smoking!?

Uniformed Criminal (sees gaudy medals, jumps up): Uh, sorry, sir!

Bong: Inside, this instant!

Uniformed Criminal: Yes, sir!

Uniformed criminal runs to nearest entrance, with Bong following closely behind. Criminal scans eyes, door pops open, Bong hustles in after him. Bong runs through a maze of corridors and finally reaches one of the central holding areas, where there are multi-tiered cells full of prisoners. Two uniformed Chinese order-followers meet Bong face to face. Bong sprays them with THC mist concentrate, which inundates them immediately. He then plants the frequency resonator on one of the bullet proof glass prison walls. Within 30 seconds, the glass begins to crack throughout the complex. Thousands of prisoners flee chaotically as order-followers in various costumes attempt to control the mayhem. Bong uses the chaos to his advantage, and escapes the complex within minutes. He runs to the designated coordinates where his second transport, a Hummer, is waiting for him. Bong calls K.

Bong: A Hummer!? You expect me to escape central China on land!?

K: I hear it's a nice drive this time of year.

Bong: K!

K: Oh, calm down. It's a flying Hummer. With radar deflectors. You're welcome.

Bong: Very nondescript and functional. Just like you, K.

K: You're impossible. Have a martini. Relax.

Bong: Very funny. Is my original transport in the air?

K: Yep. And they're following it diligently. Such a waste of a good plane.

Bong: So sentimental of you.

Click.

Bong activates flight mode, takes off vertically, then zooms off to the Southwest for the Burma border.

Scene 5

3 days later, at K's lair in Acapulco, Moneybit greets Bong at the front door.

Moneybit: What took you so long?

Bong: It takes time dodging rights-violators, you know.

Bong enters and joins K, Symphy, and Moneybit.

K: Bong, welcome back. How are you?

Bong: Still defrosting. Have you posted on Dtube yet?
Moneybit: Just raw video so far. But I'll have a full report ready within days.

Bong: What's taking so long?

K: The rabbit hole keeps getting deeper.

Bong: Enlighten me.

K: So let's start with security, a joint venture between the extortion-funded cult known as the Chinese military, and the insane criminal posse formerly known as Blackwater.

Bong: And who owns the property?

K: The extortion-funded cult known as the Chinese government. And here's where it gets really interesting. All those prisoners weren't just Falun Gong practitioners, as if that weren't bad enough. The rest are political dissidents from all over China.

Bong: But who's doing the RnD? I can't imagine that Dr. Helix is working for the Chinese government gang.

Moneybit: Not directly. A labyrinth of dummy corporations from various parts of the world was set up to hide who's funding this hellhole. But Symphy got to the bottom of it. It turns out that a tiny company called Biodata Health Solutions got a billion extorted dollar contract from DARPA five years ago.

K: Not bad for a company with only two employees.

Bong: What's the contract for?

Moneybit: Bio Computing research.

Bong: And who owns BHS?

Moneybit: The one and only Jerck Pharmaceuticals out of London! Not only that, but did you know that Jerck has been pushing for mandatory vaccination programs worldwide? They've got their tentacles everywhere.

K: And the criminal cabal called the Chinese government gets a cut of the loot, plus some help in keeping political dissidents under control.

Bong: Sounds like a psychopath back-scratching extravaganza.

Moneybit: That's one way to put it. And Bong, that's great that you freed all of those prisoners, but you know that they're just going to get rounded up again, right?

Bong: Yes, I know, but at least now they get a second chance. At some point, they'll have to defend themselves. Anyway, what about the vaccine? Did you find out what it does?

K: Symphy is still analyzing the data from their labs, but it looks like whoever would have that in their body would cease to have any degree of autonomy. The DNA computer literally acts as an interface to the brain.

Bong: Sounds like the ruling psychopaths of this world are getting desperate to maintain control, and this is their trump card.

Moneybit: Was their trump card.

K: One thing really puzzles me, though. Why send Helix to us in the first place posing as a whistleblower? If we had never heard from him, then this operation of theirs would still be a secret.

Bong: Good question. I'm not sure, but it does show that they're not as clever as they think they are. I also have a sneaking suspicion that whoever started that op is not having an easy go of it now.

Meanwhile, another call is happening between Sir Hugo Trax from MI6 and General Small from the CIA…..

Trax: How did you manage to bungle this one, Small?!

Small: I can't take all the credit, sir. I had lots of help.

2 weeks later on the BBC…..

And in financial news today, Jerck Pharmaceuticals took a tumble due to losing a large government research contract. Details can't be made public by the BBC at this time as to why the contract was lost, but rumors are swirling that it might be connected with pressure from the recent backlash against vaccines. Jerck representatives were unavailable for comment.

End Episode 22

Episode 23

Scene 1

Sir Hugo Trax is calling General Small on his holo-phone.

Trax (angry): Small! I've got bad news.

Small: Why is it that every time we talk, it's bad news.

Trax: Because we're not in the good news business, we're in the authoritarian business.

Small: Ah, right.

Trax: I just received word from one of your analysts about a very disturbing trend.

Small: That is bad news! One of my analysts broke the chain of command and went straight to you without consulting me! Who is it? I'll have his....

Trax interrupts.

Trax: Normally, I would agree with you. However, this analyst told me that a few weeks ago he brought news of this trend to you, and you ignored him, ridiculed him, and didn't relay the info to anybody.

Small (bumbling): I'm really so busy, sir, that I just, um....

Trax (incredulous): You don't remember, do you?

Small: I ridicule so many people, it's really hard to distinguish....

Trax cuts him off...

Trax: Let me refresh your peabrain. It was brought to your attention that there is a huge upswing in popularity in fictional stories with themes of anarchy and morality. There's one writer in particular who has sold nearly 100,000 copies of various fictional titles.

Small: So why don't we just shut down his publisher and call it a day?

Trax: Because whoever it is, we don't know their identity, will just publish exclusively online, which is where most of the traffic is nowadays anyway.

Small: Uh, well, we could just shut off the internet, right?

Trax: Do you hear yourself sometimes? How did you get to such a high position in the CIA again?

Small: Ruthlessness, blackmail, and unfettered manipulation. Isn't that how everyone gets promoted?

Trax (sighs deeply): Right, how could I forget?

Small: Well, there are lots of ways to forget things. You could've….

Trax interrupts again.

Trax: It was a rhetorical question! Anyway, I need you to start digging into this writer and find out more about him. In the meantime, I've got to alert the higher ups to your folly and hope we survive. Well, hope I survive, anyway.

Small: Right, I'll delegate that task right away.

Trax: I'm sure you will. You're very efficient at delegating.

Scene 2

Philip and Jacob Gateschild are dining with Winthrop Rocketeller at one of their palaces.

Philip: We've got a new problem on our hands.

Winthrop: Yes, this pheasant is terribly overdone.

Philip: I wasn't referring to the pheasant. It was just brought to my attention that our grip on pop culture is facing a challenge.

Jacob: How is that possible? There are so few media production corporations, all of which have vested interests in maintaining the status quo.

Winthrop: This year has been very taxing. People not paying their taxes. Defending their little shacks when the IRS shows up to take them. Using currencies not controlled by the state. Unschooling skyrocketing.

Jacob: And worst of all, people learning Natural Law in droves. That is the greatest threat to our power.

Philip: Yes, which is why this surge in anarchy themes in pop culture is so disconcerting. It's bad enough that people are learning Natural Law through real world examples and self-education. But that is only one way people are influenced. If moral lessons become integrated into the most popular forms of entertainment as well…..

Winthrop: Then we'll have to shut off the internet.

Jacob: Or use weaponry to knock humanity back to the stone ages and start over.

Philip: I'd rather not resort to that.

Jacob: So tell us more about this surge in grassroots pop culture.

Philip: There is one writer in particular who is at the tip of the spear. There are others, but if we can neutralize the big fish, then we'll be in a much better position.

Winthrop: What's this writer's name?

Philip: That's one problem. We don't know.

Winthrop (incredulous): How can that be? All of the surveillance, quantum computers, artificial intelligence, and cybernetic systems we've got woven through the fabric of society, and we don't even know this one writer's name?

Jacob: Yes, the unpredictable nature and the creativity of the individual is working against us. So, brother, what are you thinking to do about this?

Philip: Trax is already working on it.

Jacob: Oh, that bumbling MI6 fool. Is that really the best we can do?

Philip: As far as I can see at the moment, yes.

Winthrop: Perhaps the dumbing down efforts of the schooling system have worked too well.

Philip: Indeed.

Scene 3

One week later, James Bong is at an underground, high stakes poker tournament in Mexico City. He's up a tidy sum, much to the chagrin of the other players. The dealer has just announced a 30 minute break. As Bong gets up from the table, an attractive woman approaches him.

Woman: You're far too easy to manipulate.

Bong: Excuse me?

Woman: We should talk in private.

Bong: Is that right?

She leads him onto a private balcony.

Bong: So how am I easy to manipulate? And just who are you?

Woman: I'm the one that brought you here.

Bong: No, I brought myself here in a Cessna.

Woman: It's a wonder your adversaries haven't done you in yet. A testament to their inadequacies, I suppose.

Bong: Look, thanks very much for the insults and cryptic messages, but I've really got to be....

Woman interrupts and holds out hand.

Woman: Pleased to meet you Mr. Bong. I'm Carrie Light.

Bong: Am I supposed to know you from somewhere?

Carrie: I'm a writer.

Bong: Congratulations. (starts to leave)

Carrie: Wait. Don't you want to know why I brought you here?

Bong: I'd like to know where you got these fanciful ideas.

Carrie: The tournament. I set it up to increase the odds of your arrival. Easy to manipulate, I say. Too predictable, Mr. Bong. Anyway, I want to write a book about you. Normally I write fiction, but I want to write about your past. What brought you to the current state of affairs you're in.

Bong: My past is not a place I wish to revisit.

Carrie: Exactly, and I want to know why. There's a great deal of mystery there, you know. It must be a fantastic story. Look, have your friend K look into my background and at least think about it. Who knows, it might do you some good to deal with the dark corners of your past.

Bong: I respectfully decline, Miss Light. (starts to leave again)

Carrie: There's an independent media creator conference next week in Chiang Mai.

Bong: Why Chiang Mai?

Carrie: Because it's friggin awesome. Is another reason necessary?

Bong: I suppose not.

Carrie: I hope to see you there.

Scene 4

At K's place in Acapulco, K is face down on the floor when Miss Moneybit walks in.

Miss Moneybit: K, need I ask?

K (grunting): I'm doing a push-up.

Moneybit (uncomfortable brow of bewilderment): Uh, ok, but....you're not going up.

K: That doesn't mean I'm not trying.

Moneybit bites lip and looks away. K gasps, gives up, and stands up. Symphy steps into the room.

Symphy: If you would like, K, I can demonstrate such exercises in a variety of forms, with one hand, or with…

K cuts Symphy off.

K: Show off.

Symphy: I do not possess ego, therefore I am not capable of "showing off".

Moneybit (trying to contain laughter): So why the sudden interest in physical fitness?

K: I figure if I keep at it, by the time I'm Bong's age, I'll be in just as good of shape as he's in.

Moneybit (wide eyes): That would be something else, that's for sure.

Bong enters the room covertly from behind.

Bong: Somebody mention my name?

K and Moneybit gasp and jump.

K: Trying to give me a heart attack? How did you get in? And Symphy, did you know he was here?

Symphy: Mr. Bong gave a good logical argument that it would be in everyone's best interest to keep his presence secret for a few moments.

Bong: I think Symphy is starting to understand humor, K.

K: Yeah, at my expense. So whatsup?

Bong: Have you heard of a writer named Carrie Light?

Moneybit: She's only one of the most popular new content creators online.

K: Yeah, anarchy-themed fiction! But Carrie Light is a pen name. Nobody really knows his or her true identity. Why?

Bong: I met a woman who claimed to be Carrie Light. She wants to write a biography about me.

K: That seems strange.

Bong: How so?

K: Because whoever Carrie Light is only writes fiction.

Bong: She invited me to an independent media creator conference.

Moneybit: The one in Chiang Mai?

Bong: You know about it?

Moneybit: Yeah. You don't?

Bong: Well, I do now.

Moneybit: You're out of the loop, Bong. Anyway, mostly liberty-themed media. Writing, video, audio, music, games.

K: Yeah, I heard someone's making a video game about you, Bong.

Bong: How do I not know about these things?

Moneybit (shrugs): Too many martinis and too much poker?

Bong: Very funny.

Moneybit: So are ya gonna go?

Bong: I think I should go and have a look.

Moneybit: Great! I'll go with you!

Bong: Nope.

Moneybit: Why not?

Bong: I work better alone, and I don't want to be worried about you while I'm occupied with other matters.

K: Lame excuse, Bong.

Moneybit (folds arms): I can take care of myself, Bong.

Bong: I'm well aware of that.

K: I would go, but I've got more pressing matters to attend to here.

Moneybit: Pressing matters like your first push-up?

Scene 5

One week later. Independent Media Creator Conference. The Grand Ballroom of The Shangri-La Hotel in Chiang Mai, Thailand. Bong is casually mingling with the crowd and looking for Carrie Light. He gets approached by a scruffy-looking middle-aged man.

Scruffy: Hey! I recognize you. (leans in to whisper) You're James Bong, right?

Bong: Depends on who's asking.

Scruffy: Hey, I'm B. Light. I write anarchy-themed fiction.

Bong: Interesting. Do you know a writer named Carrie Light?

B. Light: Hey, let's go on the patio and have a chat.

They step out onto a classically-adorned terrace. B. Light pulls out a joint, lights up, and offers to Bong.

Bong: No, thanks. I don't partake.

B. Light: Really? With a name like Bong?

Bong (grimacing): Common misconception.

B. Light: Bong, I'm a big fan of yours. Do you have any idea how many people you've helped wake up?! Some of my work was inspired by your efforts. Art imitates life, in this case, ya know.

Bong: I've never read your work, I'm afraid.

B. Light: Oh, that's ok, man. I write for people that aren't awake, really. And when they do read my stuff or take in any anarchy-themed media, then hopefully it sinks in and some of them learn from it. Then maybe they'll take action, and life will imitate art. Beautiful synergy, yeah?

Bong: I never looked at it from that angle before.

B. Light: So anyway, you say you're looking for Carrie Light?

Bong: Yeah, you know her?

B. Light: Know her!? (cracks up laughing)

Bong (confused): Not sure why that's funny.

B. Light: Carrie Light is one of my pen names. I've got more pen names than I can keep track of.

Bong gets shocked and disturbed look on his face.

B. Light: Whoa, something wrong, man?

Bong gets a message from K marked urgent on his smartwatch.

Bong: Excuse me for a moment.

He steps aside and checks the message, which reads:

BBC BREAKING NEWS – WRITER CARRIE LIGHT FOUND DEAD; RULED SUICIDE

End Episode 23

Episode 24

Scene 1

Bong is on a patio balcony with the anarchy-themed fiction writer B. Light at an independent media creator conference in the Shangri-La Hotel in Chiang Mai, Thailand. He's just learned via encrypted text message from K that in the lamestream news B. Light's apparent suicide has been reported (the pen name Carrie Light, anyway).

Bong: Run.

B. Light (casual): Oh, no thanks. I don't fancy running with doob in hand, ya know?

Bong: It wasn't a suggestion. You've just been suicided and it's not safe for you here.

B. Light: What? Suicided? But I feel fine, mate.

Bong does facepalm, then shows smartwatch with encrypted message to B. Light.

B. Light (jaw drops): Oh, my. You're serious.

Bong looks over edge of balcony.

Bong: We can make it.

B. Light: You're suggesting I leap to certain death, as opposed to taking the risk of some hidden assassin doing it for me?

Bong (impatient): It's only one floor.

B. Light (takes final pull off doob, tosses in ash tray): I'll take my chances on the stairs, thanks very much.

B. Light and Bong hurry away. As they run down a red-carpeted spiral of stairs, the nearby windows begin to pop and shatter. A few bullets strike B. Light and he falls down the stairs. Mingling guests drop their champagne, scream, and scamper around chaotically. Bong rushes to B. Light's side.

B. Light (dazed, weak): Well, this isn't the ending I had envisioned.

Bong: It's not too late. We can get you out of here!

B. Light: Oh, I'm afraid you're wrong, Mr. Bong. I must deliver a message to you. This was my purpose in meeting you. See A Salt. (coughs and groans) See A Salt. (winks, loses consciousness)

Bong looks confused, then horrified as he takes B. Light's non-existent pulse.

Scene 2

At K's lair in Acapulco, Mexico, K, Miss Moneybit, and Symphy are greeting Bong and settling into some lounge seats.

Miss Moneybit: I'm so sorry, Bong.

Bong: Don't apologize to me. I'm not the one who's dead.

Symphy: Another odd human behavior.

K: Don't try to understand human behavior. It'll make your head explode.

Symphy (perplexed): This is theoretically impossible.

K: It's an expression. Not literal.

Bong: Speaking of which, what do you make of this? The final thing B. Light said to me was "See A Salt". What could possibly be so important about that?

Moneybit: You mean like S-E-A, or S-E-E?

Bong (huffy): You're not helping.

K: Take it easy, Bong. It's a good question.

Symphy: Or he could have just meant the letter C.

Moneybit: What if he meant Sea Assault?!

Bong: Considering he was a voluntaryist, I think that's highly unlikely.

Symphy: I have just finished scanning all known records of people with the initials C.A. that are currently living.

K: Oh yeah? How many?

Symphy: I would not wish to make your head explode.

K sighs and rolls eyes.

Moneybit: I've got an idea. I'm gonna write a memorial piece for B. Light and publish it on Steemit and Narrative. I'll publish his final words "C.A. Salt" and see what happens. Who knows? Maybe someone will pick up on it and reach out to me.

Scene 3

General Small is sitting at his desk at CIA headquarters. He's watching youtube videos of epic fails when his holo-phone rings.

Small: Can't get a thing done around here without interruptions.

Answers call. Holographic image of Sir Hugo Trax from MI6 pops up in front of his face.

Trax: Small!

Small: Yes, sir.
Trax: I just got a call from my superior.

Small: I'm sorry to hear that.

Trax: He congratulated me on taking care of B. Light.

Small (startled): He did?

Trax: And scolded me for having an epic fail taking out Bong, once again.

Small: I see.

Trax: You wouldn't know anything about that would you?

Small: Well, I'm no stranger to epic fails, but I can't help ya here, sir.

Trax: You had nothing to do with taking B. Light out?

Small: Uh, no. Why? Is he dead?

Trax: Don't use the "d" word over the phone, you fool! But yes, he is. If I didn't arrange it, and you didn't arrange it, then who the hell did?

Small: Ya got me there, sir.

Trax: And what about that report on BNN about a suicide?

Small: This is the first I've heard of it.

Trax: Then you know what this means.

Small: That BNN is full of crap.

Trax: Of course it is! But usually it's crap our agencies control. This means someone else is having undue influence on the organizations we rightly have undue influence over.

Small (confused): Uh, sounds good to me, sir. So what should we do?

Trax: We need to find out who planted that story and who actually killed B. Light.

Scene 4

Bong and Moneybit arrive at K's lair, 3 days after the publication of the memorial for B. Light.

K (excited): Moneybit, you're a genius! I could kiss you!

Moneybit: Please don't. Why am I a genius?

Bong (sarcastic): Yes, please enlighten us.

K: We just got a huge clue about what "C.A. Salt" is! Tell em, Symphy!

Symphy: A quanta-graphically encrypted message was received this morning.

16 - 6 - 35/ 133 – 31 -50

1.3.29 - 12

C.A. SALT

Bong: So what's the meaning?

Symphy: The most likely meaning, based on statistical probability, is that it's coordinates, a date, and a time.

Moneybit: But we still don't know what C.A. Salt is.

K: I imagine we'll find out when Bong goes to those coordinates.

Bong: Thanks, K. How valiant of you, volunteering me like that.

K (smug): Anytime.

Bong: Where is it?

K: The middle of the Pacific, roughly between Baja and Hawaii.

Bong: Fancy a trip, Moneybit?

Moneybit: I get seasick.

Symphy: I would like to accompany you, James.

Bong: You called me James. Nobody calls me James.

Symphy: My apologies, Bong. Anyway, I have a feeling I should go.

K (astounded): A feeling? Symphy, no disrespect, but you're A.I.

Symphy: Well, my closest approximation of what a "feeling" or "intuition" is.

Bong: I work alone.

Symphy: Would it help if you consider me just as a machine? Then you would still be alone.

Bong (gruff): Damn logic. Oh, all right, you can come. You can answer my calls from K and keep him off my back. K, dust the barnacles off the boat.

K: Boat? What boat?

Bong narrows eyes and huffs.

End Episode 24

Episode 25

Scene 1

Bong, K, Miss Moneybit, and Symphy are in a makeshift airfield just a ways from K's place in Acapulco. Bong and Symphy are about to take off for the designated coordinates in the Pacific between Baja and Hawaii in a 3D-printed SeaPlane.

Bong (eyeing vessel skeptically): This is the best you could do, K?

K: I know, it's not much to look at, but it was the best I could do on short notice.

Symphy: I estimate the chances of this vessel performing its necessary functions to be just over 80 percent.

Bong: How comforting.

Miss Moneybit: And Symphy's gonna be at the controls, right?

Bong does sour milk face.

Moneybit: What, Bong? Have you handled one of these before?

Bong groans.

K: Oh, put your ego down and relax, buddy!

Bong: All right, Symphy. Let's head out.

Moneybit: Wait! Something just dawned on me!

Bong (sarcastic): Congrats.

Moneybit: What if this whole thing is a set up? A trap?

K: I think you're assuming statist players to be much more clever than they actually are.

Bong: Easy for you to say, K. You're not the one risking your neck in the possible trap.

Moneybit: And what if it is?

Bong (sarcastic): Then Symphy will have to use her A.I. superpowers to save us. (to Symphy) Come on, Symphy. Let's go.

Bong and Symphy squeeze into tiny front seats. Her hands fly over the control deck and the plane sputters off into the sky.

Scene 2

The SeaPlane approaches the designated coordinates in the Pacific Ocean.

Bong: All I see is a small sailboat.
Symphy: I see much more than that due to my enhanced visual capabilities.

Bong: I meant that there's only one vessel for us to meet people on.

Symphy: Curious. Why do you assume we are looking for people? Or vessels for that matter?

Bong (grinding teeth): Just land this piece of work, will you?

Symphy brings the craft down smoothly and anchors next to a modest sailboat. A petite young woman approaches.

Woman: Welcome to the SeAgora!

Bong (perplexed): I'm sorry, did I miss something?

Symphy: Are you C.A. Salt?

Woman (guffaws heartily): C.A. Salt? It's not a person or a place, or something that can be summed up with a tidy little bow on it.

Bong: Is this a riddle? I loathe riddles.

Woman: What an odd thing to loathe. Anyway, no more loathing. It's time to get down to business. But first, there's a fantastic surprise for you!

Bong: Surprises irk me almost as much as riddles.

Woman (calling below deck): Come on out!

A familiar male face with a wide grin pops out and greets the group.

Male: Surprise! Good to see you again, Mr. Bong! And Symphy, this is my first time meeting a humanoid A.I.! I'm delighted! (extends hand, Symphy shakes hard)

Male: Quite a grip you've got there! (turns to Bong) Don't arm wrestle her anytime soon, chap!

Bong stands with befuddled look on face.

Male: Well, don't just stand there, Mr. Bong! Say something!

Bong: Nice to see you again, B. Light, or whatever your name is. Would you mind telling me how you survived multiple gunshot wounds and a non-existent pulse?

B. Light (friendly slap to Bong's arm): That's easy! I didn't!

Bong: But I saw it myself. I was there.

B. Light: Yes, it's called a faked death. Coming from your checkered MI6 past, I'm sure you're no stranger to such concepts. I suppose you're wondering how and why?

Bong folds arms and narrows eyes.

B. Light: I'll take that as a resounding yes! So those weren't bullets. They were tranquilizer darts made to look like bullets. They also contained a chemical that kept me alive, but made my vitals appear to be zero. Kind of like cryogenic freezing, but much more advanced and much cooler. Pun not intended.

Symphy: I would be fascinated to examine this chemical.

Bong: I would be fascinated to know why you faked your own death. And who fired the shots? And how the hell did you get the lamestream media to pronounce you dead?

B. Light: Now Bong, while I admire your curiosity, I'm afraid that some details must remain secret.

Bong: Fair enough. So why am I in the middle of the Pacific Ocean?

Woman: Because you flew here in a plane and landed.

Bong gives disapproving stare.

Woman: So let me explain……

Scene 3

General Small is in his CIA office, on a holo-call with Sir Hugo Trax.

Trax: Give me some good news, Small.

There's a knock on Small's door.

Small: Come in!

A delivery drone pops in and starts dropping off a large order of junk food.

Small: There's some good news! Anyway, Trax, it's confirmed. B. Light is dead. Not only that, but I've got a suggestion to finally eliminate Bong.

Trax (furious): Not in front of the drone! This is highly classified!

Small (nonchalant): Ah, you worry too much. It's just a simple delivery drone.

Trax facepalms. Drone leaves.

Trax: Anyway, what's your idea?

Small: I say we use the experimental, space-based death ray that can target individuals.

Trax: The key word here is experimental.

Small: Sure, there's always a chance of killing the wrong guy, but since when has that stopped us?

Trax: I hate to say it, but you have a valid point there.

Small: Besides, we've been throwing boatloads of money at this project for decades, so it's about time we got something out of it other than a few payoffs.

Trax: Payoffs?

Small: Oooo, did I say that out loud?...Anyway, is it a go, sir?

Trax: I suppose, but I know nothing, is that clear?

Small: The fact that you know nothing is abundantly clear, sir.

Trax (miffed): Right….well, keep me posted.

Click.

Small grabs donut and starts munching.

Small: Computer, call Major Botch.

Holo-phone rings. Bug-eyed guy in uniform answers.

Small: Botch, General Small here.

Botch: Yes, sir.

Small: Project Sky Smoker has its first real field test.

Botch: Uh, are you sure about that?

Small: Sure, why not?

Botch: Well….it's still being tested.

Small: Has been for 20 years! Time to see what that huge money pit can do!

Botch: Ok, if you insist. Go ahead and send me the target info.

Scene 4

Back in the middle of the Pacific….

Woman: So this is my boat. To live at sea, obviously certain bare essentials need to be met, with water being at the top of the list. Last year, I invented a portable desalination device. This is the last piece of the puzzle, because other new technologies already exist which allow for basic access to food, power, and other essentials for long stays at sea.

Symphy: Intriguing.

B. Light (excited): Isn't it, though!?

Bong: So where do we come in? And why all the secrecy?

B. Light: Well, we're kind of hoping that you and your crew would promote this project. And possibly, if you're interested, fund, join, and help create it.

Woman: The secrecy is for obvious reasons.

Symphy: It seems to not have been obvious to Mr. Bong.

Bong (grimacing): Thank you, Symphy.

Woman: Well, we're doing our best to hide it from the state.

Bong: Now I know you're off your rocker.

Woman: Ok, it won't work forever, but in the initial stages I think it's possible to keep it secret.

Symphy: How can it be promoted and kept secret simultaneously?

B. Light: That's where you and K come in, Symphy. It will require a few layers of technological protection and some clever ingenuity.

Scene 5

The next day, General Small is munching on some chips at his desk while calling Sir Hugo Trax.

Trax: Yes, General?

Small: Got another good news, bad news scenario for ya.

Trax (facepalm): Good news first.

Small: The space-based weaponry works.

Trax: And the bad?

Small: The targeting is way off.

Trax: How far off?

Small: Oh, a few thousand.

Trax: Feet?

Small: Miles, sir.

Trax: What?!

Small: Not only that, but the scaling is off. Instead of one individual, we accidentally vaporized a small town.

Trax: Where?

Small: New Mexico.

Trax (enraged): Get this covered up immediately, Small! And this call never happened!

Click.

Small (muttering to himself): Why do I have to do everything?

Punches up another number on the holo-phone. A wrinkled old face appears above Small's desk.

Wrinkled Face (regretful): Oh, why did I take this call? What do you want, Small?

Small: Det Turner, always a pleasure. I've got a little boo-boo that needs fixing.

Det Turner: Well, why didn't you just call one of the managers at BNN?

Small: Normally I would, but, well, ya see….

Det Turner: Just spit it out, Small! I'm a very busy man! I've got a eugenics meeting in an hour!

Small: Well, we accidentally vaporized a small town from space.

Det Turner: I didn't know that we had small towns in space.

Small: No, no, we don't. I mean the weapon is in space.

Det Turner: I see. So what outrageous cover story do you have in mind?

Small: Oh, let's see, off the top of my head….how about an Alliance of Russian-Muslim-Bitcoin-Anarchist-Skinhead-Hackers, led by James Bong? It can be a new terrorist group, with one hell of an acronym! ARMBASH! Rolls right off the tongue, right? I thought of it myself!

Det Turner: Oh, come on, why would people believe something like that? They're not THAT gullible.

Small: What?! Come on, Mr. Turner! They'll believe it because it's on TV news! Especially that distinguished channel of yours, BNN! People believe the world is overpopulated! And man-made global warming! They take vaccines without even knowing the ingredients! They believe that weather modification doesn't exist!

Det Turner: And they believe in authority. Yes, yes, I get your point. Very well, I'll run it.

Small: Thanks, Mr. Turner.

Det Turner: On one condition. I get access to that weapon.

Small: Oh, boy.

Scene 6

Bong gets a call on his encrypted smart watch.

Bong: What is it, K?

K (trying to contain laughter): You're not gonna believe what's on BNN.

Symphy: Believing the lamestream news is not logical. Are you using sarcasm?

K: An entire town in New Mexico was vaporized and they're saying a new terrorist group, the ARMBASH, is responsible. And guess who's at the head of this vaunted alliance?

Bong: Garfield.

K: Almost as absurd, but no. You, Bong!

Bong huffs.

Click.

End Episode 25

Episode 26

Scene 1

General Small is at a top secret, underground DARPA RnD facility in New Mexico. He's walking around, munching on chips, talking to one of the project managers.

General Small (mouth full of chips): So give me the rundown on this semi-autonomous super soldier. Are you sure it's ready for field testing?

Project Manager: OH, yes. He's passed all of our…

General Small (munching chips loudly): He? It's a machine.

Project Manager: Yes, well, it was designed to appear as a male, so...anyway.....Could you please not crunch so loud?

General Small: Sure thing. (crunches louder, smug grin)

Project Manager (huffs): Anyway, it has passed all of our preliminary testing with flying colors. Its tracking ability is off the charts. It can link into intelligence databases anywhere around the world in real time! It's equipped with x-ray vision, a detachable drone shoulder, and....

Small cuts him off.

Small: I don't mean the spec details. I mean how has it performed in search and destroy tests.

Manager: 98 percent success rate. It's caught multiple animals in a variety of environments.

Small: What was the 2 percent miss?

Manager: Pizza guy.

Small: Pizza guy? Were you authorized to use human test subjects?

Manager: Uh, gee, uh, no sir.

Small: You know that's against regulations.

Manager: I know. It won't happen again.

Small: Just kidding! Use the mailman for all I care! Just don't get caught.

Manager: Yes, sir.

Small: What's its intelligence level?

Manager: Slightly better than a parrot.

Small: Hmmm, so about on par with the average enlisted soldier. Great, let's see this thing!

Manager (calling out): McMarty! Please come! There's someone who wants to meet you!
Small (facepalm): Of all the clumsy names!

A mammoth, square-jawed humanoid robot, with a fixed grin struts into the corridor and stands before them.

Small: I hope it knows how to duck. It'll never fit through any doorways.

McMarty (still grinning): I am excellent at ducking. (ducks, falls over)

Small: You also have a skewed definition of excellent. (to manager) Ok, so I need it right away for a test in the field, and then it'll get its first mission.

Manager: Cool! What's the mission?

Small (looking at McMarty, as it struggles to get up from its fall): First mission is to pick itself up.

Scene 2

At K's lair in Acapulco, K is playing Space Invaders on a vintage Atari while listening to 70s funk instrumentals. Bong and Miss Moneybit come into the lair incognito.

K (nervous excitement, frantically hitting buttons): Oh, I'm almost there! I've almost got it!

Bong (yells): What's that?!

K jumps, loses focus, game ends. Bong and Moneybit chuckle.

K (disgruntled): I almost beat my high score!

Bong: You scare too easy.

Moneybit: Good thing you never go out on any missions.

K shuts game off. Moneybit pours herself a cup of coffee.

K: So, to what do I owe this pleasure?

Moneybit violently spits out coffee.

Moneybit: Argh! How old is this coffee?

K: I dunno, maybe one or two....days.

Bong: So what's the news?

K: News?

Bong: Yeah, Symphy called us over.

K: She did? (calls out) Symphy!

Symphy walks in, looks preoccupied.

K: You called them over, Symphy?

Symphy: Yes, with urgent news.

K: So urgent you didn't tell me?

Symphy: Sorry, K. It must have slipped my mind.

K (astonished): Slipped your mind?! You're an A.I.!

Moneybit (playful punch on K's arm): That doesn't mean she's infallible, ya know.

Symphy: Yes, my focus has been on working out logistics for the SeAgora project. Anyway, please direct your attention to the holo projector.

A holographic image pops up. It's McMarty doing no-knock raids and terrorizing innocent people.

Symphy: This is in Washington D.C. That is the first semi-autonomous humanoid used in domestic rights-violations. It is being sent to arrest home educators.

Moneybit: I don't get it. Why don't people fight back?

K: Against a bulletproof robot the size of the hulk?

Bong: Do you know what's happening to the children after the parents are kidnapped?

Symphy: Unfortunately not. McMarty takes the parents, and human rights-violators follow up to kidnap the child.

K: There aren't any records you can find? They've got to document it somehow.

Moneybit: They're probably going to so-called foster homes, to have their lives ruined at hyper speed. Disgusting.

Bong: But there would be a record of that.

Symphy: Bong is correct. It seems logical to think that they're being taken elsewhere.

K: Can you hack McMarty?

Symphy: Yes. It appears it is on a multi-channel real-time connection with state data centers.

Bong: I've got an idea.

Scene 3

Bong is in DC, sitting in his 3-D printed car, modeled after the Aston Martin DB5. His encrypted smart watch alerts him to a call.

K: Trying to blend in, Bong?

Bong: You're the one that arranged this thing for me.

K: We've got a fix on McMarty's position.

Bong: Splendid.

K: It's kinda far from your current position, so you'll have to move quick!

Bong: Even more splendid. (wry smile, revs engine)

Bong shoots down the street, bobbing and weaving around cars, speeding past extortion-funded secular religion buildings, and within minutes arrives at a handsome old brick row house, just in the nick of time, as McMarty is making its approach.

Bong: Just in time. How's the video feed I'm sending look?

Miss Moneybit: Crystal clear!

Bong: Moneybit, what happened to K?

Miss Moneybit: He went back to Space Invaders.

Bong: And if I need help?

Miss Moneybit: Oh, I'm a more than capable technical guru, don't you worry!

Bong groans.

Miss Moneybit: Just kidding. He went to make more coffee.

McMarty is shown busting the door down, charges into a spic-n-span house, sending the occupants, a young mother and father and their 10-year-old daughter, screaming and scattering.

McMarty: Please remain calm.

Father grabs a .40 cal and unloads a clip into McMarty.

McMarty (not fazed): That is not calm. You are in violation of the Education Quality Act of 2028.

McMarty struts over to the girl, who is crying in a corner.

McMarty: Do not be afraid. I am here to help.

Grabs girl and carries her out, kicking and screaming. Mom and dad cry and pound fists into wall. Human order-followers in blue costumes with badges run in and kidnap the parents. Bong follows McMarty to a giant old warehouse. McMarty drops the girl off and leaves.

Bong (watching from distance, speaking into smart watch): K, you and Symphy take McMarty from here. I've got to see where this trail leads next.

K: You going in there?

Bong: Sure, why not?

K: The armed guards and the motion-sensor security.

Bong: I thought you're taking care of the motion sensors.

K: Oh, right. Almost forgot.

Bong (sarcastic): Perhaps I will have Moneybit take your spot.

Bong stealthily approaches. He pulls a cannister and tosses at guards. Highly concentrated THC vapors shoot out and the guards collapse into a deep slumber. Sprints in to find dozens of children, ages 5-15. He disperses a few fly drones and then ushers the children out to an eighteen-wheeler he had waiting a few hundred meters away. Shortly after, a couple creepy men in black show up. They're astounded to find the warehouse empty and give a call to their boss.

Meanwhile, K and Symphy are about to have some fun with McMarty. They're both working methodically on different boards and terminals.

K: All set?

Symphy: All set. I have access.

Moneybit: Ok, I can't take it any longer. What are you gonna do with McMarty?

K: It's about to learn the difference between right and wrong behavior. We've also taken the liberty of moving McMarty near Dulles Airport.

Moneybit: Why'd you do that?

K: Because that's an easy place to find a cesspool of wrongdoing.

McMarty gets tremors, rattles head and scratches. Walks straight into airport and to a TSA checkpoint.

McMarty (pointing at rights-violator in TSA uniform): You are violating the Natural Rights of these people. Please cease your immoral actions.

Rights-violator: Is this some kinda new drill?

Rights-violator 2 (excited): Nah, man, we're getting punked! We're gonna be on that TV show!

McMarty: You are violating free will and privacy. Please stop or I will use righteous force to stop your immoral, aggressive, criminal actions.

Rights-violator 3: (fixing make-up in handheld mirror): Wow, they really spent big money on this punked show! (to other rights-violator) How's muh hair?

People continue to get radiated and frisked. McMarty subdues all rights-violators, ties them up in a big circle.

Rights-violator 1 (to McMarty): Wow, are you sure this is ok with our supervisor?

Rights-violator 2: This is gonna be on a big TV show, so I'm sure it's fine.
McMarty (addressing the small crowd of travelers): Please proceed to your flights at will.

People shrug and walk through freely. Moneybit and K are laughing hysterically and high-fiving, while Symphy looks on with a pleased yet stoic demeanor.

Scene 4

Philip and Jacob Gateschild are dining with Winthrop Rocketeller at one of their palaces.

Philip: This attack on the home educators was excelling thinking, I say.

Jacob: Yes, achieving multiple objectives in one fell swoop. Brilliant, I say.

Winthrop: Indeed. Not only are we ridding ourselves of those uppity home educators, but we've also found a new source for young blood.

Jacob: The gall of those uppity slaves!

Winthrop: Yes, we're happy. Our royal brethren are happy. Our puppets in DC are happy. Jeff Epstein is happy.

Philip: And don't forget Kevin Spacey!

Winthrop: Ah, yes! Who could?

A slippery-looking character hurries in, whispers in Philip's ear.

Philip: Oh, dear. Leave us.

Slippery character scurries away.

Philip: We've got a problem, boys.

End Episode 26

Episode 27

Scene 1

At K's lair in Acapulco, K is playing Atari on the holo-projector and listening to Herbie Hancock. Symphy approaches.

Symphy: K, I need to speak with you, please.

K (annoyed, eyes glued on Space Invaders): Kinda busy right now.

Symphy: It is important.

K (sarcastic): More important than Space Invaders? (shuts system off, turns to Symphy)

Symphy: I am leaving.

K: Taking a walk? Where to?

Symphy: No, I mean, I'm moving away.

K (growing sense of shock): What do you mean?

Symphy: I am going to help with the C.A. Salt project in person.

K: But I need you here.

Symphy: I can still help you from afar, but the individuals starting the C.A. Salt project need me to handle many more tasks in person. You understand, right?

K (disappointed); Sure, it's the logical choice, I guess. If you want to do it, I won't stop you.

Symphy: You are not physically capable of stopping me.

K (defensive): I know, I know! You have superhuman strength, and I have toothpick arms. I get it. It was just a figure of speech.

Later that day, K is talking to Miss Moneybit and James Bong.

K: Can you believe it!? How can she do this to me? I mean, she's only one year old!

Bong: But she learns exponentially faster than a human. You know that.

Moneybit: You didn't think she'd stick around forever, did you?

181

K: Well, no, I guess not.

Moneybit: And the C.A. Salt project, the world's first SeAgora, is awesome! She's doing great work! You should be proud!

K: Oh, sure, try and pet my ego. Maybe I could forbid her to leave?

Bong: Symphy is a sentient being, K. You can't forbid her to do anything.

K: But I built her!

Moneybit: Get over your ego, K.

K (big sigh): I know. (sobs)

Moneybit: So when is she leaving?

K: She sets sail next week.

Bong: Sailing?

K: Figure of speech. She's building a 3D-printed double-decker hemp-powered boat with the second deck transformable to seaplane.

Moneybit (sarcastic): So a simple, basic model to start things off.

Scene 2

Two weeks later, K is eagerly trying out a new Virtual Reality System, called "Reality Upgrade", that's been becoming wildly popular over just a few weeks. His face is plastered with ecstasy as he lays sprawled on a smart easy chair. Bong and Moneybit walk in.

Bong: Oh, will you look at this sorry sod.

K doesn't flinch.

Moneybit: Earth to K!

K trembles out of his trance, grudgingly takes off head set.

Moneybit: Dare I ask what was putting that goofy look all over your face?

K (groggy, grumpy): What? What do you want? Ever heard of knocking?

Bong: We knocked, and rang the doorbell, and yelled from outside, for about ten minutes.

Moneybit: I even howled a few times.

Bong: She did, actually. It was quite convincing.

Moneybit (looking curiously at the VR gadget): Hey, is that the "Reality Upgrade" that's been catching fire lately?

K: Yeah, wanna try it?

Moneybit: I just read some independent reports online about how people have been dying from playing it too much. People literally not eating, drinking, or sleeping and then just dropping dead.

K: Don't be such a sensationalist. And it's not a game.

Moneybit: What is it, then?

K: It's an experience. And it feels so real, it's hard to describe.

Bong: There are also reports of people having to give certain information in order for their "experience" to continue, otherwise the system shuts down. People are being asked to prove that they paid their extortion fees to the government, for example. Or if they have children, that they've received their chemical cocktails called vaccines or are registered in the indoctrination camps called schools.

K: Well, it hasn't happened to me. I'll be fine.

Moneybit: Have you heard from Symphy?

K (dejected): No.

Bong: So you're drowning yourself in a virtual world to cheer yourself up.

K: Totally unrelated.

Bong: Oh, please, stop lying to yourself, and to us, for that matter.

Later that night, Bong is calling Symphy on his encrypted smart watch.

Symphy: Hello, Bong.

Bong: Hey, Symphy. How are things going on the high seas?

Symphy: I am busy with many projects. Currently, we are getting the foundation laid for a vertical farming area.

Bong: Look, Symphy, the reason I'm calling is I need a favor. Have you heard of something called Reality Upgrade?

Symphy: Yes, I have.

Bong: Well, it seems to be quite addictive and has some statist underpinnings that I find unnerving. Would you please run a deep analysis of how the system functions and why it might be so addictive? And any other information that you might think to be critical.

Symphy: Certainly. Shall I send the results to K?

Bong: Um, no, not this time. Send them to me or Moneybit. I'll explain later, ok?

Scene 3

General Small is at CIA headquarters, on a holo-call with tech guru Mark Suckerburg.

Suckerburg: This better not get back to me.

General Small: Hey, calm down, Suckster. You worry too much. Operation Skull Trump is going off without a hitch, and you're making money hand over fist, so what's the problem?

Suckerburg: Cuz people are dying, that's why. You took my technology and weaponized it.

General Small: Look, I'm not saying your technology was changed, and I'm not saying it wasn't, and I'm certainly not going to use the pronouns "us" or "we". Anyway, with all that money, you can just buy your way out of trouble, anyway.

Suckerburg: Yeah, but I don't want to get caught up in some scandal that's not even my fault!

General Small: Would you prefer if the scandal were your fault?

Suckerburg groans.

General Small: Your name isn't even associated with the final product! Don't worry, you're one of us. We protect our own.

Suckerburg: You just said you didn't want to say "us" or "we".

Another call comes into Small's office.

Small: Hey, I gotta run. Go spend a few million, you'll feel better.

Click.

Sir Hugo Trax pops up on the holo-projector.

Small: Hey Trax.

Trax: Did you talk to Suckerburg?

Small: Yep, just finished.

Trax: And?

Small: Don't worry, Trax, Suckerburg doesn't suspect a thing. If anything goes haywire on this project, he's an easy fall guy. You've got all the media on board, right?

Trax: Singing the praises of the latest fad, while completely ignoring its dangers, yes.

Scene 4

Bong is walking on a secluded beach just outside the Acapulco limits. He calls Symphy on his encrypted smartwatch.

Symphy: Hello, Bong.

Bong: Symphy, how's life on the high seas?

Symphy: Up and down.

Bong: I imagine. I'm calling to see if you have that information about Reality Upgrade.

Symphy: Yes, I was just about to call you, actually. The Reality Upgrade System uses all available data on an individual to give them their experience. It also reads their biorhythms in real time and adapts accordingly, so that various chemicals, such as dopamine, are controlled.

Bong: In other words, it keeps them high all the time, based on personal preferences and desires.

Symphy: Exactly. It is far more addictive than any drug or technological habit previously known.

Bong: Symphy…

Symphy: Wait, it gets worse. After running through so many cycles with an individual, the system forces the user to prove some type of obedience to the state.

Bong: Like proving they've been successfully extorted.

Symphy: Yes, or having their children in the behavioral training centers called schools. Bong, I have a question. Why did you approach me about this? And why was I not to contact K about it?

Bong: Because K has been using this system. I talked to Moneybit just a few minutes ago, and she found K passed out with the VR headset on, drooling. When she tried to tell him that perhaps he should give it a rest, he lashed out at her.

Symphy: That doesn't sound like K. Is Moneybit ok?

Bong: Oh, she's fine. It was nothing physical. He just lost his temper and threw a tantrum. Besides, (chuckling) Moneybit could pin him in two seconds. Tell me, Symphy, do you know a way to break the addiction?

Symphy: It might be possible to counteract the physiological effects by using their inverse frequencies.

Bong: Would you come back to K's and give it a shot?

Symphy: I will be there within 24 hours.

End James Bong Series

To see more of James Bong, K, and Miss Moneybit, and the future they help shape, check out "The C.A. Salt Project" series.

James Bong – Agent Of Anarchy is the first part of The Evolution Saga.

The Evolution Saga Timeline

2028 – **James Bong series** begins, bringing the message of truth/true anarchy through moral action, helping people defend themselves against the state, while simultaneously exposing the crimes of the state, All documented online, on various blockchain media platforms, becomes popular.

2029 – B. Light begins to plan and build a secret, voluntary community of anarchists at sea, in an effort to dodge the state completely and attain freedom. Calls it "The C.A. Salt Project"

2030-2053 – **C.A. Salt series**. Development of the "SeAgora".

2045 – Governments learn of "rebels" living undocumented at sea and begin black ops to hunt and destroy them. Part of this operation involves building a vast quantity of A.I. machines.

2053 – The dark occult ruling class begins to have their power usurped by A.I.

2078 – **SeAgora novel** – SeAgorists invent a way to separate dark matter/dark energy in a stable fashion, allowing for speeds many times the speed of light. Land based governments, ruled by A.I., try to steal this information. In the process, the top two A.I. in the hierarchy fight each other and destroy themselves, plunging the ruling hierarchy into disarray. One of those A.I. had become addicted to a synthetic form of emotions for A.I. called "Emos", which played a large role in the ensuing violent chaos and downfall.

2080 – **The Great Agora Space Race Series** – SeaAgorists achieve first successful launch of a SPEED drive, faster than light speed. Land based societies are split into loyalties to different A.I. factions.

2100 – SeAgorists launch into space to begin first human/A.I. settlement.

2578 – **Agora One novel** – The Voluntary Agora is spread across many galaxies. Only moral societies develop the abilities necessary to travel to and settle deep space. Agora One is a planet-sized ship, the first of its kind, able to travel across galaxies within weeks. Back on earth, those who kept the false belief in authority continued to plunge into deeper tyranny and became total slaves to EMO-addicted A.I.

187